CONFRONTING SATAN AND THE EVIL DYNAMIC

In American Politics & Life

I0664526

By
Jeremiah Stubbs

Table of Contents

Introduction

I am very confident that this small book provides very big insight, and more wisdom than any other book you will ever read relative to the fundamentals of good, evil, and man's ethics distinguishing what is considered right from wrong in political and religious reasonings, which governs the subsistence of life and people everywhere on earth.

The time has come for humanity to confront the beast of conflict, destruction, and senseless death in the world. It is without question that this topic is very unorthodox and original in its context, because as far as I know, no other author has ever addressed this issue from the specific line of reasoning as discussed here.

We all know that evil exists, but the specific problem that I am centering on is that society has failed to make the evil dynamic a separate and distinct issue for public education or public scrutiny so that people are more astute of Satan outside of religious edification. Without a much broader and expansive approach to education in this regard, Satan and the evil dynamic will continue to be shielded from realistic detection or political

1

accountability. This is despite the fact that the power and supremacy of Satan is working daily in the mindsets and lives of the very souls we elect to control the quality of our livelihoods through the political process, right now, today!

A major issue prompting the writing of this book concerns the fact that the evil dynamic is without any restriction in its catastrophic potential to harm us, while masses are currently suffering, homeless, sick, and dying all over the world in the absence of any challenges to stop or to hold the evil dynamic accountable. There are no checks and balances in the psychological or psychotic evil that is running wild and rampant in the thinking of key people who are placed in extreme positions of power and influence, who are consequently given rights to lawfully harm us without any answerability.

There must be a way to stop and to prohibit such unrestricted evildoing for the sake of peace, which is what is most important at the end of the day. Peace is the most important aspiration sought after by people from all over the world, despite whatever religious ideal any race may embrace. We need peace, and so long as there is no peace, there will always be conflict and war. There will always be controversy and unrest. This book is about facing the truth, challenging, and confronting Satan to his face to hold him accountable by moral ethics and righteous principles ordained by the Creator. We must come to the realization that Satan is only as powerful as we ourselves make him based on our own fears, worries, doubts, and unrealistic apprehensions. Satan is nothing but a weak fool who preys on the fearful, the vulnerable, and the ignorant who are without understanding of his inferior nature incomparable to God the Creator. It is these two dynamics; good & evil, from which every element of human existence and survival rests. We must study these dynamics and reach conclusive understandings how they fit into each of our lives relative to our eternal joy or sorrow.

I reason that Satan, the forces of evil, and immoral people who are captivated by satanic influences, are real tangible concerns not to be taken lightly, as is customary practice in American culture. The tangibility of Satan's existence is evidenced by the actual effects of his harmful ethics and principles that are daily administered everywhere in life by evildoers clothed with political authority.

Because America have separated the affairs of the Church from the State in its' ethics of political reasonings, we have substantively hidden, minimized, and abandoned the relativity of God, Satan, and the substantive nature of the good and evil

3

dynamic from everyday public scrutiny, which are the most two important factors governing life and the subsistence of humanity everywhere. It is important to realize this! It is to Satan's advantage to separate himself from the Church. That way, he will not have to be held accountable to moral scrutiny and righteousness.

As a consequence, there are no safeguards anyplace in the nation to delimit the power or control of Satan and the evil dynamic, which is an actual being that is aggressively operating in the invisible spiritual/realm, from where Satan is with the influential spiritual power to possess, to control, to persuade, and to manipulate the minds and thoughts of weak, unsuspecting, and vulnerable souls who are not protected or saved by the mercy and grace of God the Creator, which is due to their own ignorant disobedience to submit to the will and principles of God as instructed in Biblical precepts.

The concern is that the politically immoral are not being detected, are not being exposed, nor being publicly denounced for who they truly are, which is because of Satan's cunning separation from the Church. Yet, they are actual culprits and evildoers who are operating under the evil dynamic; most who are empowered in political offices and perpetrating the works of depravity and injustices at the behest of Satan and his spiritual angels -(Demons). These are the primary people causing all the chaos, destruction, and senseless death in the world. These are the people whom this book confronts with truth that exposes who they really are at the end of the day.

I clearly realize that to some, this dialogue sounds a bit strange, as far as speaking about things of the spiritual nature that are unseen with the normal naked eye. I realize there are countless people who don't believe in things that they cannot see, touch, or feel. There are millions upon millions of people in the world who don't believe or trust that the spiritual world truly exists. Many skeptics count the assertion of God, Satan, and spiritual matters as foolishness, insanity, or assert that those who believe in such things are misled or mentally challenged in some manner.

There was a time that each of us once held unbeliefs and skepticisms about spirituality and things we could not physically see. But with time, experience, trial, and error; we eventually mature, we learn, and we grow up to accept new realities and understandings. If you don't believe in the spirit world, then this book may not be for you. This is because I reason that the entire essence of existence is manifested from the spiritual world, which holds the key to every relevant matter going on in the physical/carnal world.

Another way to consider this analogy: think about the power of one little mustard seed. Take that seed and consider that seed to be one of your concentrated thoughts. In other words, perceive the seed and your thought to be equivalent to each other. The seed is not the mustard tree yet. It is just a seed without anyone being able to see any of its fruit, because it's just a seed, with the same power to manifest as a thought can also manifest. Your thought is just your thought, just as a seed contains the same power as your thought. You may be thinking of building a mansion, but the mansion has not yet been developed, produced, or brought into reality; it's just a thought at first. But in that thought there is potential to build the mansion just as you see it in your imagination. Likewise, just as a simple seed is just a seed without any evidence of any mustard tree grown yet, but has the potential to grow a tree.

Finally, the seed is planted in the soil, which is equivalent to your thought being planted in your mind. Your mind and the soil have the same potential. Your mind is the soil that could grow/produce into reality any thought you plant in it; just as everything in life grows from the soil through the seed. Just as the soil, everything that man has ever invented and still inventing on this earth is first produced in the mind, which is based on his thoughts, which are the seeds of manifestation.

Okay, so after the seed is planted and given water and sunlight from the universe, it starts to produce evidence of growth, which is equivalent to you giving daily imagination and faith to your thoughts. Your imagination and faith is like the sun and the rain. A plant cannot grow or manifest anything without the sun and rain, despite being planted in good soil. And neither can your thought/mind grow or manifest anything without imagination and faith in your ideas, which are substantively your potential seeds. In due season a mustard tree grows into physical reality where it could be seen with the naked eye. This new growth is equivalent to your idea of a mansion finally being completed and now seen in the tangible/physical material world. Initially, both the seed and the thought were void, without form, without substance, or without any tangibility.

This is indicative of how the spiritual world works, except for God is the only spiritual force behind both the seed and the thought through His laws, power, dominance, superiority, and control of the universe which contains the water, the soil, and all the natural resources that keeps both the seeds of the earth and the thoughts of man afloat on the earth. This is why we all need God! No one could sustain life without God because God only produces the good things that keep us all alive. To the contrary, Satan, who is just the opposite of God, produces only bad things to oppose all good things, which assures us pain and death. It is the evil spiritual dynamic that is the cause of all our problems in the world. In neither case, can we actually see the good dynamic nor the evil/bad dynamic with the naked eye because they are spiritual realities. Though we know they exist, we cannot see either physically!

For this reason, the spirit world is more superior than the physical/carnal/material world. This is because everything had to first come from the spirit world before it could manifest into the carnal/physical material world. Our thoughts are spiritual! In the beginning there was a word, and the word represented a thought. And that thought contained potential power to manifest itself, which is how God manifested life itself in our present carnal world. And because God made man in His image, man can also create anything on earth he desires by his words likewise. But first, words must be initially implanted in your mind, starting with a thought, an idea, a vision, a dream, or some imagination aimed at manifesting it into reality. They are all spiritual realities with potential to be, but not yet produced. The formula for those spiritual realities to manifest, is to have enough faith to the point where you could intelligently see those things as if they already were. At the end of the day, your mind is the key, which is the seed with the capacity to create anything you desire, so long and you can see it in your imagination.

This is the reason why it is so important not to allow Satan to possess, to enter into, to control, or to influence your thoughts. You are capable of being influenced, misled, fooled, tricked, deceived, bamboozled, and so forth. This is how Satan eventually controls your mind. You don't want this to happen because the end result is never good because Satan's influences are the opposite of those things that are good. The outcome is never productive, is never beneficial, and is only harmful and destructive; meaning that you will eventually become harmful and destructive yourself for conforming to Satan's course of life in any capacity. This is what the churches and religions are metaphysically saying to us at the end of the day.

If you are mature and intelligent enough to understand that there is a spiritual world aside from the carnal world, then I am confident that you will understand the contextual implication that I am making here, relative to Satan and the evil dynamic. If you don't believe in the spirit world, then I would suggest that this material is not for you. But I would encourage you to make efforts to understand the underlying essence of what I am attempting to convey, because it is for your own good and wisdom. Research information and gain knowledge of the spirit world, and afterwards you will gain a much clearer understanding of spiritual matters and become much wiser in all areas of your life in the carnal world.

Despite any religious faith, this book concentrates on the evil dynamic, and attributes this dynamic to whom the world recognizes as Satan the devil, who is the author of all confusion and evildoing. This hypothesis argues that the evil dynamic and the forces of Satan should be a matter of public education and scrutiny aside from mere religious teachings or philosophy alone, of which I reason is the cause for Satan's overwhelming superiority over the affairs of humanity.

Even if you don't believe in God, you nor any other person walking upon the face of earth can deny that the good and evil dynamic does exist, and that each carries with it the actual power to either help or to harm each of us. These dynamics are relative to our thinking and the nature of our thoughts, which are the basis of our values, our decisions, our behaviors, and are relative to our perspectives on life, which is basically everything about you and the seeds your have implanted in your minds throughout life that has ultimately brought you to your current fate.

If someone of whom you trust persistently tells you that you should not drink any water because all water is bad; you may eventually stop drinking water; provided if he or she convinces, persuades, or influences you to believe such nonsense. These are the key words: convince, persuade, influence, and believe. This is what it takes to bring people under one's control, which is how Satan and the evil dynamic works to overcome the minds and lives of millions of people around the world. Once you are persuaded to believe in a thing, you are programmed and destined to act accordingly. This is why it is important to guard your mind from any negative, evil, or immoral people. This is also why you should watch the company that you keep, because perception and belief imbeds power beyond one's direct awareness, understanding, or control.

Let's say you actually believed the absurd assertion that all water is bad and should not be consumed. Eventually you will find yourself developing health issues based on such poor advice. At the end of the day, that advice resulted from mere words conveyed to your mind of which you thought about, accepted, and believed to be true. Those words have power. That power has influence, and that influence affected your thoughts to the point that you believed what you were told. And based on that belief, your behavior was shaped to conform to the false assertion, leading you to a false conclusion not to drink water, which is to your detriment instead of your for your wellbeing. At the end of the day, Satan has conquered another soul to conform to the dark world of lies and confusion. The Bible says that Satan is the author of confusion!

This is because it was untrue and bad advice, it was wrong and amounted to a bad influence, resulting in a harmful result. Because that advice is harmful, the advice was wrong, which only belongs to the evil dynamic ruled by Satan the devil. Why? Because it is untrue, because it is destructive, and because of its harmful nature. Any and everything that is harmful comes only from Satan. This is how Satan works. It is his nature to lie, to deceive, and to eventually bring harm and ruin in our lives by any means necessary. Satan only harms at the end of the day.

If you were to carefully look into the life of a person who would give such poor advice not to drink water, you will find that such a person is somehow influenced by Satan. Why? Because he or she is spreading lies and laying a foundation for one's destruction and death. Whether they did it deliberately or not, such people have been misled and have fallen for the lie, of which only Satan implants in the lives of others; hoping that you or I will eventually fall for the trap, and we ourselves ensnare others based on the lie. He is the master of lies and deception. Satan needs fools, lazy, dumb, and gullible people who are easily misled to do his dirty work for him. The advice not to drink water was from a person who lacked diligence to learn the facts, to study, to ask questions, to make sure they knew what they were talking about before spilling their unfounded opinions on others. This is the sign of a gullible person, a thoughtless person, a careless person, and an immoral person led by the evil dynamic. Satan uses these types of people all the time. The world is full of these blind souls.

The Good dynamic, ruled by God, does just the opposite of Satan. God represents the truth. A person of God will give you the right advice that is only helpful. If a Godly person tells you the truth about water, you will drink water and gain all of the benefits it has to offer to your body, which will only help you at the end of the day because it is the most precious thing ever to be consumed by the human body. God's advice is positive and healing, while Satan's advice is negative and harmful.

This is an example of how the evil versus the good dynamic works. They are spiritual realities, which are actual forces relative to the intellectual reasoning of thoughts, words, information, ideologies, opinions, perspectives, education, and any facet of knowledge with the capacity to sway your mind and behavior to do good or evil deeds. There are good thoughts that correspond with good behavior, and there are bad thoughts that correspond with evil behavior. The evil behavior induces pain, trouble, and eventual harm. The good dynamic is just the opposite, which produces good behavior that is healing, trouble-less, and eventually helpful to someone or for some cause. Because nothing good in this world could ever harm you, all good is the way to go!

At the end of the day, these are ethical principles of spirituality that dictate whether you are a moral or an immoral person, which is based on your good or evil reasonings in life. One, the good dynamic, is definitively right because it helps us, which is what every person alive wants. And the other, the evil/bad dynamic, is definitely wrong, because it harms us, which is what no one wants anywhere in existence. These challenges and dynamics will be with mankind forever!

Because these dynamics are not standard ethics of ordinary societal education, aside from church and schools of Theology; the predominating masses are confused, oblivious, and remain vulnerable and unable to control the inevitable injustices that are destroying the fabric of human relations and man's quest for peace and happiness everywhere on earth; all because of Satan and the evil dynamic. I reason that these dynamics should be basic understanding through ordinary education so that people will remain alert, conscientiously aware, and daily prepared to defend against the evil forces that Satan will utilize to hold us in bondage to sin through various tricks and schemes.

If we were to institute new standards of education to teach about the fundamentals of Satan and the evil dynamic outside of religion standing alone, society could reposition itself to delimit, to prohibit, and to utterly stop Satan and the evil dynamic from attaining any power and/or control over the political affairs and fate of the nation any longer. In doing this, we could assure there would never be another Donald Trump or any other of his kind, who are indecorously governing the affairs of this great American nation without showing any love, compassion, or justice, which are the cornerstones of morality and righteousness for the good of all people.

Trump has demonstrated that he has chosen the evil dynamic, which is self-evident from the harm and injustice that he clearly demonstrates in his policies and political reasonings. This is why

15

it is time for the society to move towards a new level of political standards relative to the spiritual nature and disposition of political leaders and others relative to whether they are good or evil natured people. This determination could be ascertained through a help or harm analysis, which is a standard method for moral review, by which to evaluate others based on the ethics and reasonings underlying one's sentiments, perspectives on life, religion, and other matters pertaining to his or her mental and intellectual acuity for human reasoning. This topic will be explained in further discussion herein.

In this book, I clearly explain every reason why the evil dynamic should be a matter of public education and societal scrutiny, unlike any other book written on the subject surrounding Satan and the evil dynamic.

The Evil Dynamic

Even though it is the most important factor that is adversely affecting the affairs of human relations, the vast majority of people on this earth simply don't pay close enough attention to the nature and essence of the evil dynamic, which is a living reality in the spirit world with the potential to dominate the thinking, the ethics, the principles, and the behaviors of the men and women who are governing our lives in America and everywhere else in the world. This is what is most important at the end of the day: the evil, and the need for mankind to subdue and bring this harmful but inferior dynamic under intelligent observation and control!

When speaking of the evil dynamic, I am talking about a spiritual force of nature with unlimited potential to imbed evil thoughts in the mindset of mankind, which are only grounded in negative energy that is destined for some facet of destruction against someone or something in the world. The evil dynamic and evildoing is manifested through hatefulness, vileness, and extreme ugliness, which only results in injustices, pain, and untimely death; which are all bad and harmful attributes that are unfavorable to the life and livelihood of mankind everywhere in existence.

17

The truth is that the evil dynamic and all of its' attributes are a derivative and work of who the world recognizes as Satan the devil. This is the one and only dynamic that we must decipher out from behind the shield of deception; cunningly preventing itself from detection, from guilt, and from intelligent exposure. It is covertly secreted behind closed doors, while conspicuously orchestrating works of depravity in the world without challenge or confrontation because of our own acceptance and failure to confront its supremacy through organized exposure. It speciously works in conspiratorial conjunction with assigned demons -(immoral politicians), who Satan has deputized to assist in his works of injustices against innocent and vulnerable victims over whom the wicked have speciously gained political authority.

According to every religious belief in existence, all agree that there is an evil dynamic in life that is ruled by Satan, who we call the devil. All religions and all nations agree in one capacity or another, that Satan is with the spiritual capacity and wherewithal to mentally and emotionally dwell in the conscience of men and women everywhere on earth, having the power to captivate and entice vulnerable and spiritually defenseless souls to fall under his supremacy; causing such misled men and women to evolve into evil and immoral people in their thoughts and deeds towards humanity. And this is the problem that we must eliminate! Collectively we must confront Satan without fear any longer. It is only by our own fear that Satan reigns with power in the world.

Satan cannot do his dirty work alone. He needs followers. He needs fools, he needs people with no dignity, he needs liars, and he needs people with no love in their hearts. He needs ignorant people, selfish people, materialistic people, greedy people, angry people, harmful people, dishonest people, immoral people, vicious people, cold-hearted people, violent people, and he needs people with no integrity. These are the people that he needs. He needs these foolish followers to join his kingdom because they possess all of his own characteristics. Likewise, these types of people gravitate to Satan because they are equally of his nature.

It is the thoughts and deeds of these immoral souls that Satan persuades, uses, and has always used to stir the conflict, uproars, unrest, division, and wars going on in the world. These are the evildoers he is using now, and are the same minds and spirits that he has enticed to inflict so much harm and injustice over past history, of which we are still seeking answers and resolutions to resolve to no avail as of yet. But there is still hope, provided we see the hidden truth secreted in the spiritual essence of this one

19

and only culprit of destruction, which is the evil dynamic that continues to keep the masses in the blind and confused. It is true that knowledge is power! And in this hypothesis, I will make the most realistic attempt possible to bring this understanding to the forefront of your understanding unlike any other author has ever attempted to do as persuasively as I will here.

Because the essence of the evil dynamic is not taught in mainstream education, it is not a separate and distinct issue by and within itself outside of religion, as it should be. For this reason, the vast majority of people are ignorant and passive to challenge the sovereignty and dominance of Satan in political undertakings. And this includes the unfortunate immobility of very intelligent people who fail to act adverse to the evil dynamic as well. It is not that this intelligent segment won't take action; it is that they don't know what action to take because there has never been any established protocol, any platform, any method, any process, nor has there been any procedure implemented anywhere in the nation to even began to focus on the concept of an evil dynamic, aside from religious education alone. However, there is always the first time for everything in life, and this book will be the first to at least think in the direction of taking new approaches to subdue the authority and power of Satan and his dynamic, as it is well rooted in American politics and culture.

We must first accept the fact that the masses in general are without a fundamental understanding of how the evil dynamic within itself is the epitome of everything wrong in the world. We must first establish this understanding as basic knowledge and realization. Second, we must accept the fact that there is no educational foundation upon which to stimulate the necessary energy, imagination, thoughts, or realization of the evil dynamic in order to counter against its destructive characteristics. We must conclusively understand that evildoing is responsible for everything that is wrong everywhere in the world. Third, we must make it an objective understanding that the fundamentals of the evil dynamic should be a separate and distinct matter of public interest and education, which should be focused upon outside of mere religion alone. Of course we don't want to do away with religion, because religion is good and needed because it instills those good morals that we all need in any case. God and Jesus are real dynamics based on evidence, experience, and the many supernatural events that were witnessed and still being witnessed by countless people from all around the globe everyday.

Relative to our political, religious, and societal differences; we tend to talk about, to debate about, and to complain about all of the evildoing, destruction, chaos, and conflict going on in the world. But we are without any realistic or objective goal to resolve our apprehensions. Yet, we utterly fail to discuss or to focus on the primary culprit behind the evildoing itself, of which I am trying to convey what we should do. We must compel common, ordinary, and everyday people, whether they are religious or not, to come to recognize Satan as a spiritual being that exists, who is the king and ruler of the evil dynamic, which manifests all harm that humanity dreads everywhere on earth.

One way or another, everyone must reach this understanding, even without religion if necessary. The point is to expose the hidden psychology behind the spiritual forces that are continually in progress relative to words, knowledge, and understanding between the good and evil dynamic, and how these dynamics are ruling the world according to which dynamic is empowered over the mindsets of those we entrust to protect our basic human rights and quality of life. It is essential that we make people understand the relevance of these dynamics.

In order to create a new landscape and perspective of reasoning that will bring us back to civility, respect, and peace in American culture, we must re-establish new codes of conduct and rationalities under the United States Constitution affirming that all human conflict, controversies, injustices, and evildoing going on in the world is only caused by immoral and evil people. It is imperative that these people be deciphered out and held accountable for implementing, for practicing, and for bringing about tribulations, conflicts, harm, or injustices that is the proximate cause resulting of their own immoral behavior, immoral policies, or immoral directives, which are detrimental and harmful to all of mankind.

The point that I am trying to make is that it is these immoralists who are the culprits of the political wrongdoings and injustices going on in the world. Without this segment, we would all be enjoying a good quality of life right now! It is only this segment who are spiritually influenced under the guise of Satan, who are compelled to create conflict, unrest, division and war in the world as a result. It is these very people who are responsible for chaos and unrest going on everywhere. But as I am emphasizing here, there is a way to stop these evildoers, if we would only acknowledge, recognize, scrutinize, distinctively categorize, and confront this immoral segment apart from the moral segment in the nation, who poses no harm to humanity as does the evil segment. There is a need for a distinction and a separation between the two dynamics, just as there is a need to separate the negative from the positive forces in order to avoid the clash, to avoid the explosion, or to avoid the repelling energy that is utterly destructive by and within itself. If this book does nothing else, it will at least give us a platform from which to build a foreseeable strategy to expunge Satan from political power and authority everywhere on earth.

One way or another, everyone must reach this understanding, even without religion if necessary. The point is to expose the hidden psychology behind the spiritual forces that are continually in progress relative to words, knowledge, and understanding between the good and evil dynamic, and how these dynamics are ruling the world according to which dynamic is empowered over the mindsets of those we entrust to protect our basic human rights and quality of life. It is essential that we make people understand the relevance of these dynamics.

In order to create a new landscape and perspective of reasoning that will bring us back to civility, respect, and peace in American culture, we must re-establish new codes of conduct and rationalities under the United States Constitution affirming that all human conflict, controversies, injustices, and evildoing going on in the world is only caused by immoral and evil people. It is imperative that these people be deciphered out and held accountable for implementing, for practicing, and for bringing about tribulations, conflicts, harm, or injustices that was the proximate cause resulting of their own immoral behavior, immoral policies, or immoral directives, which are detrimental or harmful to others in the nation.

The point that I am trying to make is that it is these immoralists who are the culprits of the political wrongdoings and injustices going on in the world. Without this segment, we would all be enjoying a good quality of life right now! It is only this segment who are spiritually influenced under the guise of Satan, who are compelled to create conflict, unrest, division and war in the world as a result. It is these very people who are responsible for chaos and unrest going on everywhere. But as I am emphasizing here, there is a way to stop these evildoers, if we would only acknowledge, recognize, scrutinize, distinctively categorize, and confront this immoral segment apart from the moral segment in the nation, who poses no harm to humanity as does the evil segment. There is a need for a distinction and a separation between the two dynamics, just as there is a need to separate the negative from the positive forces in order to avoid the clash, to avoid the explosion, or to avoid the repelling energy that is utterly destructive by and within itself.

Both Satan And God Should Not Have The Same Rights Under The Constitution

Despite this understanding, we have allowed both the negative and positive forces to enjoy the same rights in political affairs. We have allowed the moral and the immoral to enjoy the same rights. We have allowed the good and the evil dynamics to enjoy the same rights. We have allowed Satan to have the same rights as God under the nation's Constitution. And this is the problem! Under the United States Constitution, which is supposed to be a peaceful document intended only for the good of humanity; Satan has inherited the same rights as God under its' Equal Protection and First Amendment Clauses, despite that everyone knows there is no good in Satan whatsoever.

Somehow we have permitted Satan to intermingle with the principles of God, and yet we complain because he is not doing anything good for humanity, despite already knowing there is no good in him. This is the very principle that has laid the foundation for the evil to stalk American culture; giving Satan equal rights under its' Constitution, which substantively gives him rights to harm us relative to his very essence and evil nature. This is because evildoing is what he does! Why are we blaming

Satan, when he is only doing what he is designed to do by his very nature? Ask yourself this question. It is not in Satan's nature to do anything good, but for some reason, we keep complaining because everything he does is harmful to us in some way. It makes no sense, because it makes no sense for us to permit Satan to have equal rights in the first place. All moral politicians should think about this truth! Why are we getting upset with the inevitable when we have voluntarily allowed Satan a seat at the table of negotiation in our political affairs? He is only doing what he is supposed to do! Don't get mad at Satan; stop him! This is why there must be a confrontation.

It is obvious that the United States Constitution was written for the good of the people, which makes it substantively a good document of God, because its fundamental nature is only intended to help humanity. Help only comes from God and the good dynamic. When carefully reviewing all of the documents' specific provisions, there is no evil intent found anywhere in the Constitution. There is nothing harmful in the Constitution. So, why would we allow the harmful to partake in its' fundamental objective? Understanding this, then why would we allow Satan to align himself with God at the expense of the life, liberty, and pursuit of happiness aspired by all men and women? We only need God be cause only God can help us! We Don't need Satan because only Satan can harm us!

I am going to say this again; because there has been no system of moral accountability ever introduced under Constitutional standards of law, requiring the immoral to face political scrutiny under the jurisprudence of America's legal ethics; the evil dynamic is otherwise with unlimited authority, with massive power, with catastrophic influence, and with unrestricted control over the livelihoods of the masses without challenge or realistic recognition for who and what it truly is. This is truly the reason for the multiplicity of problems and issues we are facing in America presently and in the past. Everyone who is concerned about the injustices going on in America and in the world should come to understand this truth. I am trying very hard to get this point across because this is what is actually happening in America and in the world today.

Another point to keep in mind, is that evil is utterly harmful. And most importantly, no one welcomes any facet of harm into their lives, which is what makes any and all harm definitively wrong. When something is definitely wrong, we all have a moral obligation to oppose such wrongdoings, whether we are directly affected or not. This is how humanitarians and moral segments react to injustices without being appointed, without being assigned, or without being hired by anyone to get involved in efforts to stop injustices, and/or to help people because of moral love and justice that is in their hearts.

Humanitarians are moral people who feel the pain of injustices and wrongdoings. Wrong is the lowest of the lowest conclusion anyone could reach about anything after all of the facts, the evidence, and the ultimate proof of assertions are summed up and adjudicated to ascertain the final conclusion of any matter. The essence of wrong is substantively saying that everything you have conclusively thought, said, or done about a matter is false, incorrect, unjust, and is not the right way. We can go no further than this truth. And when the truth is established after all factors are considered, justice has finally been met and concluded! And people want and deserve justice on all levels of livelihood at the end of the day.

The problem is that although the truth has been established after weighing and evaluating all of the facts and evidence proving that Satan and the evil dynamic is definitively harmful and wrong, such As Donald Trump and his cohorts, there are some people who won't accept the results or the truth of their wrongdoings, despite the evidence and the truth is patently clear to any reasonable person.. Again, why would Satan agree that he is wrong, when we already know that he is the king of liars? So, even though we clearly see and understand the harm and the injustice of Trump and his comrades, just because he persistently claims that we don't know what we are talking about and that he is right; we are limited in what we can lawfully do to enforce justice because there are no other lawful means or countering arguments that opposing political factions can make because the United States Constitution is without any other provisions of law to stop the works of Satan. This is because he has been given the same rights and authority under the Constitution that was only intended for the good dynamic under the principles of God, which is the only dynamic that can help us all.

This is what is truly happening in America, whereas the people clearly understand the evil, clearly see the evil in an immoral President, but is only minimized in their efforts to stop him by merely complaining and pointing out his wrongdoings without any other foundation for justice. But despite that he understands this, he still won't budge from his self-centered disposition. Instead of persistent bickering and complaining, we must face the reality that Satan will not accept the truth, he won't accept the evidence, and he won't accept the facts that prove the ugly truth of his harmful nature. Despite hearing the repetitive cries for justice, he still continues to inflict injustices and harm in the world without mercy or conciliation for any of his wrongdoing. And this is the problem! He feels no shame for the harm he causes. He feels no remorse. He feels no sympathy. He thrives from the infliction of pain, misery, sadness, deprivations, and unending conflict. Yet, we have placed Satan and God on the same throne under the nation's Constitution. We only have ourselves to blame.

The Essence Of Harm Is Humanity's Biggest Concern

It is the harm that people are fighting against in this world at the end of the day that gives credence, purpose, and substantive cause to oppose the agendas and causes of immoralists, such as Trump and others, who slimed their way into political offices, seeking to harm selective groups of people, rather than helping all citizens. Because all of mankind seeks and needs daily help over all other things in life; those who are inflicting any facet of harm against others are natural enemies to humanity, which happens to be immoral people influenced under the evil dynamic. They are the literal evildoers, clearly recognized by their harmful deeds alone, without need for more evidence to validate who they truly are among us.

Stop and actually think on this note for a brief moment: Satan exists, the evil dynamic exist, immoral people exist, moral people exist, God exist, and the good dynamic and its' attributes that are governed by God alone, all clearly exist in the kinetics of life. When we look at these fundamental principles, when we look at our daily experiences, and when we look at the basic practicalities of life itself relative to these proclamations; we intelligently see that all of these statements are true without the need for religious philosophy or further persuasion. This is because we continue to see and to experience these truths for ourselves everyday. And also because mankind everywhere in existence have experienced these truths time and time again over the course of history through trial and error. On each and every occasion the one and only inevitable truth continues to show us only one set of irrefutable facts: that all evil harms us, while all good helps us.

These are not mere statements; these are breathing living facts! So, we have help from the good dynamic, while we have harm from the evil dynamic. The moral and just will choose help, which is good and comes only from God Who is all good, and Who only created all good things. That is the wisest choice. That's the choice I am going to ride with, and it is the choice that all moral people choose to ride with. But there are also moral people who are inclined to ride with the good dynamic who are being tested everyday to convert to the evil dynamic. This is why the Bible tells us to stay alert, cautioning that Satan walks to and from the earth seeking whomever he could devour or to entice.

As I have emphasized, it is only because we don't customarily educate about the evil dynamic or scrutinize the essence of these truths throughout our societal relations or in public schools, why the nation has become numb, insensitive, and oblivious to see or to understand these truths relative to the influential impact that Satan has on those we rely upon to uphold justice and equality in political affairs. We must also keep in mind that as a result of such massive oblivion of the evil dynamic, as hypothesize in this book, the very essence of Satan and his influential authority amongst the mentality of evildoers in political offices has been shield from detection by the masses, which holds them from accountability by default of societal ignorance to investigate the spiritual essences of the good and evil dynamic outside of religious indoctrination and influence.

Unfortunately, it is for this above reason why Satan has been shielded from both realization and from scrutiny, although dwelling and diligently working in the mindsets and lives of immeasurable evildoers under his command everyday, who are currently dominating both political and economical power in American and in the world, under which authority defenseless and vulnerable people are undergoing devastated harm without any protection.

Another thing to realize, is that all of the controversial issues and the actual mental, emotional, and physical damages themselves that Satan causes amongst the masses in the nation, are nothing more than annoyances and distractions to keep us fighting against ourselves and unfocused on the truth about what is really going on behind the scenes of injustices. Today these injustices are speciously manifested and being carried out by Satan's immoral servants (evildoers)- operating in political government under the agendas of the Republican regime. This is what we must keep in mind at the end of the day! These people are literal agents of Satan, and we must start calling them out for who they truly are. We can intelligently identify these people based on the harm they cause relative to their policies, their statements, their sentiments, their objectives, and by scrutinizing their political agendas where there is no help on behalf of all the citizens at the end of the day.

We must stop merely complaining about the problems and harm that the evil dynamic causes, and start focusing on and confronting Satan's very essence and existence, with an understanding the he is substantively behind all of the problems of which we complain in the first place. This hypothesis argues that we should focus on and confront Satan and the evil dynamic with aims of expungement. And we do this by advocating and pursuing realistic resolutions that will bring this evil entity to the forefront of mass attention, where collectively we can successfully eradicate the evil dynamic from political authority. As one collective body of moralists from all over the world with a focused and concentrated mission, nothing can stop us from eradicating those immoral and harmful segments -(evildoers)- working against us in political government under Satan's authority. Collectively, we can accomplish this goal by identifying, by discussing, and by intelligently strategizing through effective and realistic pro and con analysis to create new laws, expanded educational mandates, and mass media discussions and dissemination of Satan and the evil dynamic's relevance and impact in political affairs and in life. The world must come to recognize that Satan nor immoral people should be afforded any rights whatsoever. In America, citizens must come to realize that the evil dynamic is the only problem we have, and that we must collectively fight against immoral segments who are clearly against justice, peace, and love for both citizens and strangers.

Otherwise, the only thing we are accustomed to doing in American culture is protesting against injustices, yet failing to identify or to realistically challenge the very essence -(the evil dynamic/Satan), who is the sole adversary behind the injustices of which we perpetually protest. What the moralists are substantively accustomed to doing throughout all of history, is rightfully blaming the immoral people for one injustice or another that infringes upon fundamental human rights of one kind or another; but yet without seeking further consequence or alternatives to do more, to go further, or to focus on workable strategies to challenge and/or to stop Satan's influential capacity all together. Otherwise, it must be taught as standard knowledge out side of religion, that immoral people are merely agents of Satan by and within themselves. They are without direct power or influence on their own accord, but live and operate under Satan and the evil dynamic's spiritual essence, directives, and possession, which permeates their thinking, their aspirations, and consequently their harmful behaviors towards humanity.

All We Have Are Our Beliefs

What we are dealing with is a spiritual warfare in this life. We are dealing with a warfare that has been going on since the dawn of existence, but without truly understanding how to get a grip on, or how to bring this force under intelligent control or submission. Outside of religious belief, the evil dynamic has existed in the world long before religion or biblical teachings ever came about. During the history and story of Adam and Eve as wrote in the Bible; there was no paper, no pencil, no technology, no established language or structured societies, nations, or political systems of government with any intellectual faculties, principles, tested knowledge, theories, or other presumptions of evidence to even suggest whether a thing is right or wrong aside from what man himself said he was told what right from wrong is.

Mankind only evolved through systems of assertions and conformity to one or another's thoughts, words, ethics, principles, or beliefs; which were instituted by the creativity of one man after another over the course of history, and then systematically passed down and accepted s facts and truth until to date. At the end of the day, all we have are beliefs, which gives justification to man's purpose. And purpose establishes a cause.

And a cause gives us a focused direction and understanding relative to that cause, from which ethics, cultures, values, ideals, education, and man's motivation to subsist with a set of principles by which to live, to conform, and by which to govern our livelihoods here on earth.

Otherwise, during the story of Adam and Eve, there is no evidence of its truth other than belief, faith, and trust that it is true and genuine. And actually, faith or absolute belief in anything has more power than the thing believed in itself. This is because the mind has more power than any matter. Remember, the mind created the matter. The matter did not create the mind! This is why Jesus said in Biblical scripture that if a person had enough faith he or she could move mountains. See, it is the faith implanted in the mind that is dominant in everything we seek to accomplish. The power lies in the faith itself. We just don't have enough of it, and most have no true understanding of it. This is key! Belief is key to manifesting everything, because before you can believe anything you must first imagine the thing, which all starts in the mind. Faith and belief are synonymous to each other, and without either of these you can manifest nothing.

This is why the mind is over the matter, and has much more power than any matter. The matter is just here. It could do nothing on its' own accord. A stone is just a stone. It is just matter. It is not going to do anything on its own. It takes a person to control the matter, and that control could only take place once the mind tells the body to take the necessary action to do something with the stone, based on the specific information, knowledge, or understanding conveyed in thought to the mind regarding whatever you desire to do with the stone. The stone is not going to take any action on its own accord. It has no power!

At the end of the day, you are your mind, not your body. Your mind is the only power you have. Your body is just a material substance without any power of its' own. Without your mind, your body could do nothing and you may as well be dead. If the mind truly believes that anything could be done, regardless of whatever it may be; wallah! It is just as well as completed. This is why Jesus put so much emphasis on faith. Absolutely every miraculous healing or other miracles that Jesus had performed according to Bible scriptures, were only accomplished because of the belief, the trust, and the faith of those He healed. That is what assured successful results without failure at any time or on any occasion relative to Jesus's miraculous performances.

At the end of the day, Jesus was able to do all of the good things that He performed because He only embraced and believed in the good dynamic, trusted the good dynamic, and strictly heeded to the principles of the good dynamic; while detesting the evil dynamic, as I am doing here in this book right now! No matter however you may look at it, all power starts in your mind. The power is within your thinking from the mind. And the manifestation of things from the thoughts deriving from your mind is the proximate result of the nature of those thoughts. Satan, of the evil dynamic; invokes, captivates, controls, influences, and dominate thoughts in the mind that corresponds with his nature, which is only evildoing. This is why it is important to understand how Satan works. His only mission is to oppose God and bring bad things into the world.

God does the opposite, which will result in doing only good works. The power is in the mind, and the manifestation of things in your life results from the information, knowledge, and beliefs that the mind believes is true, which is the embodiment of the faith of which Jesus so often emphasized. If the mind accepts a thing as truth, even if it is false, you are bound to gravitate towards that thing, and will be inclined to manifest your destiny based on that belief. This is how and why some people have so many crazy and mentally deranged habits and material things in their lives. Just imagine how many minds that Satan has captivated to his advantage, and is still captivating millions of minds as I write!

This is the basis of this analogy! It is to advise that you only want to put positive, good, productive, righteous, and moral thoughts into your mind and spirit. Because these good attributes will be the manifestation of your destiny. These are the good attributes and fruits of God the Creator. There is no other word in existence that is more powerful than just the mere word good standing all alone. Without this one single word, nothing good will exist on earth; not even you or me. This is why it is good to only put good things into your mind, which could only come from God, Who is synonymous to the word good.

Understanding the power of your mind, and realizing the potential power of either Satan or God to captivate the persuasive capacity of your mind is of utmost importance. This is because you could be persuaded to follow either dynamic and wind up being either a moral or an immoral person. I choose morality, while many choose immorality, which is from Satan and the evil dynamic. This is the wrong dynamic because of its innate harm and destruction of all good things. I give the highest credence to Biblical teachings because scripture rightfully disputes, detests, condemns, and oppose the evil dynamic to the utmost. In fact, the entire Bible is in direct contradistinction to Satan and the evil dynamic. It is written specifically to oppose the evil dynamic. And its' entire purpose is to persuade, to convince, to encourage, to warn, to demonstrate, and to intelligently tell mankind to oppose Satan and the evil dynamic.

The problem is that most people cannot grasp the overall fundaments of the Bible and where it is actually going, relative to perceiving the Holy Book from a metaphysical perspective of reasoning. But this is what the book is really all about after the dust settles. It is about exposing and challenging Satan and the evil dynamic with a warning, and encourages a way of life that instills integrity, morals, principles, and the servitude to help each other in some capacity. It assure us that love and peace amongst humanity is good for the human and pleases God, rather than the hate and war that continues to devastate the quality of human life everywhere that pleases Satan and the evil dynamic.

It is because I can see that a relevant segment of people are confused, uncertain, have been misled, misdirected, are simply lost about what the Bible means, or have unwittingly embraced other religious and spiritual ideals in efforts to find substantive purpose and meaning to life; why I am compelled to share my God-gifted insight and wisdom on this issue. Too many people are confused, are misled, are without a true understanding, and are without a realistic perspective about the Bible or life itself, relative to the good or the evil dynamic. Consequentially, this enormous segment of the masses are defenseless, and are consequentially ensnared by the forces of Satan, who is truly the master of all confusion.

Despite that some may disagree, Satan is a tangible force that actually exists just as you and I exist, but not in the physical form. Just as we have a mind that will exist forever, far after our bodies stop working, which is called death; the mind of Satan is alive as well. Except for Satan has the influential power to use other people's minds and bodies to do his dirty work for him. He incapsulates himself in the minds and souls of unwitting victims, and uses their physical bodies to his advantage once he has successfully implanted the fruits of his wicked thoughts into their lives. Once he has control of the thoughts, which is where all of the power lies, you become him. This is how you should look at how Satan works.

None of us are our actual bodies, nonetheless. We are our thoughts, our mind, and our beliefs. At the end of the day this is all we have, because it is only by these that we are prone to do anything we do in this life. Our mind and our beliefs are all that we have. And whatever knowledge, information, ideas, or perspectives permeate your mind, those attributes determine your behavior, your fate, and your eternal destiny. You don't want to conform to or fall prey to the controlling knowledge, ideas, or perspectives of the evil dynamic ruled by Satan, because that will be your portion and your destiny, which is eternal pain and torment in what we call hell. This is because of Satan's harmful and painful nature. This is what hell is all about. It is a spiritual reality relative to the principles of cause and effect, just as in the carnal/material-physical reality, we recognize and respect the saying, "What goes around, comes around." Or we can say it is "Karma."

You Create Your Own Destiny

The conceptual understanding of Karma is universal law that is within a perimeter of an understanding all by and within itself, and need no interpretation because it defines itself based on the actual trials, errors, and consequences experienced by mankind ever since his existence on this earth. Everyone discovers this truth at one point or another in his or her life based on actual experiences and the resulting counter-effects that we each encounter similarly to our experiences over the course of our lives. There is a cause for everything we do in this life and there is an effect resulting from that cause that cannot be avoided. This is what is recognized as Karma. It is an invisible force that carries an inescapable principle with an intelligent warning that is far beyond the confines or control of mankind, which substantively says that,"*If you don't want something unfavorable to come into your life, then don't distribute such unfavorable thing, regardless of whatever it is, into the lives of others. And if you do, you will experience equivalent or greater pain and suffering than the harm or pain you caused others to experience.*

In other words, Karma is a silent and self-evident justice that is destined to occur or to return in the life of any person according to the very choices and behaviors that he or she may have made over the course of their lives adverse to others, of which principle equally applies to any individual born anywhere on this earth whatsoever. This is the reason why I have a saying, "There is no escape from wrong!" No one gets away with anything in this life without paying a price in some way, shape, form or fashion. And it is only Satan who could induce us to bring this harm to ourselves and to others. So, it is our job to stop him to the best of our ability.

It is true that the Bible has already predicted Satan's fate, but the Bible did not say everything because knowledge is infinite. Knowledge never stops. Jesus may have said enough, but He did not say everything, because the vast spectrum of knowledge, the multiplicity of words, different understandings, new discoveries, inventions, new ideas, and ever-expanding studies in science and technology presents proof that there is no end to knowledge or understanding. We have accepted what we have been given, and have only built from that limited understanding, irrespective of the fact there is much much more to learn, to discover, and always more to understand in this life. But the principles of the good and evil dynamic will never change, despite how much we learn, no matter how many new inventions we create, and no matter how we may change our lifestyles. Knowledge is infinite, but the dynamics of good and evil are two principles that will remain forever.

We have wisdom, insight, foreknowledge, and discernment, which enables us to do anything in this world we desire to do. And even after reaching what seems to be the impossible, there is still more for us to learn, to discover, to invent, and to make infinite innovations and concepts of life, science, and technology. At the end of the day, we actually know nothing, other than whatever new knowledge, beliefs, opinions, ideas, or perspectives that are indoctrinated into our thinking and feelings, of which we either accept and conform to, or reject and go in a different direction according to our own beliefs and perspectives. It just so happens that there are more followers than leaders in the world. There are more people in the world who need leaders, than powerless followers. Leaders set standards for the followers. And if a leader's standards are founded upon evil principles, then the followers will result to being a bunch of evildoers living under the leadership and standards of corrupt politicians or others with ideals stemming from the evil dynamic, which is nothing more than Satan himself in the spirit. This is how a corrupt family, a corrupt society, or a corrupt nation is birthed at the end of the day! It is the good or evil nature of the leaders themselves that is most important after all is said and done. It is the negative, evil, and corruptible thinking in the mindset of a leader that determines the resultant practicalities in culture, education, and traditional standards of a society or nation under immoral leadership, that deems an evil society or nation.

In the midst of all this conversation, there is still even a bigger issue at hand relative to the evil dynamic that will rationalize the entire purpose why we fight against Satan in the first place. This concerns the ultimate harm that is fundamentally and intrinsically imbedded into the very DNA of the evil dynamic, of which no one wants or welcomes into his or her life anywhere in existence, of which only Satan alone can cause, but only through the adverse behaviors of others.

The people that Satan uses to do his dirty work in this regard could actually be recognized according to his or her deeds at the end of the day. Our deeds are a reflection of our moral or immoral nature, because deeds are either good or evil. There is no in between. Either you help or you harm at the end of the day. If someone is harmed in any way relative to one's deeds, no matter in what manner; such a person and his deeds are only of Satan the devil. Why? Because of the harm, which only causes pain that no one welcomes into his or her life anywhere.

49

Everyone rejects pain, which is why everyone should reject Satan and the evil dynamic because there is nothing helpful about the evil dynamic.

People are only looking for good things and help in life, because nothing good will ever harm anyone. This is why it is important to learn that harm only comes from the evil and bad element that is successfully ruled by Satan. This is the only proof we need to identify what is what and who is who at the end of the day. This very understanding is how we should decipher out who the evildoers are amongst us in the world, and not just in America alone. By analyzing and detecting whether there is any harm involved in any matter is enough evidence standing all alone to tell us everything we need to know about a person, about a group, about a society, or about a notion. Just by simply evaluating the very essence and nature of harm being done to others by itself; anyone should be able to determine the good or evil nature of a person, and to morally assess his or her moral or immoral value to humanity. This is because God harms no one, and whenever harm is present, Satan is present, the evil dynamic is present, and the dirty work initiated by Satan's immoral servant/s have completed his or her task to manifest some facet of harm against you and others in the world. These are the evildoers who are responsible for all of the harm going on in the world.

At this point of intelligent reasoning in our modern-day history, we already know with certainty that absolutely nothing good in this world could ever harm anyone, and that absolutely nothing evil or bad will ever help anyone with anything. These truths are universal understandings and natural laws of God that are very intelligently confirmed through Biblical scripture and other spiritual philosophies. These truths have been affirmed ever since the dawn of intellectual perception, wisdom, and understandings on all levels of reasonings and rationalizations known to the human mind! Yet, people who have empowered themselves in political offices under the Republican Regime seem to have somehow missed out on this understanding.

The only way that anything good could ever harm you, is if you yourself abuse a good thing, which does not make the good thing itself the cause of the harm. The resultant harm is because of your own overindulgence, or because of your own misuse of a good thing, which is called sin. Overindulgence is sinful because it falls under the passions of greed and gluttony, which are sinful qualities deriving from the evil dynamic itself. I recall having this discussion with a friend who disagreed, and reasoned that good things can in fact harm us. He reasoned that the processed foods and drinks containing tons of toxicities and chemicals are good tasting foods, but are harmful to the extent that some of these foods have caused many deaths.

It really sounded like a very good argument, but without substantive rationale. I responded by simply advising him that it is only the good elements in the processed foods and drinks that is keeping us alive. I then reasoned that if you were to remove all of the good elements from the food and drinks and only consumed the chemicals and toxic elements put into the food, you would surely die in a very short period, which his true. And likewise, if you were to remove all of the bad chemicals and other toxic elements from the foods and drinks, not only will you live, but you will be more healthier and live much longer. This is proof that nothing bad can ever help us in any way, shape, form, or fashion; while everything good will only help us. The bad elements and toxicities put into the good food is the only reason why people have health issues. The adverse health issues is not because of the good in the food; it is the bad element that was put into the good food, which in turn has a bad effect on the health of whoever eat foods that contain toxicities and chemicals. Even those toxicities and chemicals are from Satan and the evil dynamic themselves. How? Because God made good things only. The bad elements put into the good food is in contradistinction to God's plan for human health and salvation.

Anything that is in opposition to any good thing is in opposition to God. This is why processed foods containing unnatural chemicals and toxicities are BAD for your health. They are bad because they are from Satan, who is the King of the bad element. This is why people are brought to early deaths who eats junk foods, which contains the most impurities. It is because they consume bad food, which is merely Satan in disguise, as he guises himself in every way that he can to snare mankind into some facet of destruction, harm, and death.

We can also narrow this same issue to down to an even more example to expose the dynamics of Satan. For example: let's look at the chemists, the agriculture industry, scientists, the Food and Drug Administration, and all others associated with the food industry. The chemicals and impurities were only put into foods because of Satan's servants. How? Because they disobeyed God's natural laws of nature, and created chemicals and impurities to make foods taste better, despite knowing that the chemicals are bad for one's health. They do this out of greed, stemming from the love of money, which a sin deriving from the kingdom of Satan and the evil dynamic. They prioritize profit over the quality of people's health and lives. They aspire for the love of money, while shunning integrity, disregarding love, ignoring compassion, and undermining righteousness. These are all sins falling under the standards of Satan and the evil dynamic; merely narrowing down to simply a candy bar that is killing your health at the behest of Satan because of its' destructive and harmful nature, knowingly catastrophic to your health, but yet promoted by unscrupulous people who has prioritized wealth over principle. The bad in all foods is because Satan has a hand in it in some capacity.

See, this is proof that we only need good things to survive, which is because nothing good will ever harm us! This includes the good natured people relative to their thoughts, values, and deeds as well. God only created good things, which is why the bad element ruled by Satan and the evil dynamic is no good under any conditions! It is impossible to ever get anything good from evil/bad.

God Himself only stands for all things that are good, Who Himself is merely a synonym of the word good, Who created only good things consistent with Biblical precepts and understandings. This is why no one on earth can live without good things, and why no one on earth can live without God, regardless of anyone's specific religion. Without God, then you are left with only one other alternative for your hopeful survival, which is to embrace Satan and the evil dynamic, which is in direct contradistinction to the sovereignty of God in every capacity of Satan's existence. There is nothing to the bad element but bad results, which only amounts to immoral, evil, or to bad outcomes of one sort or another, of which no one wants or welcomes anywhere. Do you see the logic that I am persistently making here?

People with bad thoughts cannot produce good outcomes in their planning of any sort. People with bad values cannot enjoy a good quality of life under no circumstances. People who manifest bad deeds cannot expect good results on no account. No matter how you may look at it; nothing of a bad nature whatsoever will ever help you or anyone else in this world with anything. Rather than utilizing the fundaments of Biblical teaching based on its specificity, what I am doing here is breaking down its fundamental implication and overall metaphysics of Christianity so that maybe you will embrace Biblical teachings and the Christian doctrine with a realistic understanding, with direction, with wisdom, with an intelligent perspective of reasoning, and with a realistic purpose to live and enjoy the beautiful quality of life while serving God and the good dynamic of existence.

Although the immoral segment -(evildoers)- poses a problem, they are not the primary problem within itself who we are dealing with. This is because these evildoers are enthralled by a captivating and possessive force outside of themselves, (the evil dynamic), of Satan, who is not being distinctly recognized or independently dealt with in more innovative ways to deter the works of Satan in the society as it should be. The primary aim is for Satan to be independently targeted, recognized, and excluded from relevant affairs of the people as a basis to stop the ongoing dilemma of chaos and destruction caused by apparent evildoers at his behest, who are secreted in high offices in America and around the globe.

People should be concerned that Satan poses a universal threat to peace, not just in America, but everywhere. As life continues to show us, all things change within time, and the time has come to approach the throne of Satan from a new angle of reasoning if we want change. But before we can intelligently do that, we must first understand how he works, how he thinks, and how he moves throughout life captivating and using others to his advantage to bring harm upon us. Throughout history, people like Adolph Hitler, Stalin, Benito Mussolini, and other dictators have left an ugly scar in history that should remind us that leadership should not be entrusted to Satan. The countless deaths of men and women over whom them they ruled is evidence enough that we cannot afford to accept evil, hateful, and very dangerous leadership any further, if we are to enjoy a peaceful quality of life.

Figuratively, we all must confess or come to understand that Satan and the evil dynamic is the primary problem, who should be called out as such through the identity of those specific evildoers among us who are captivated under his influence and operating in governmental affairs, where the American people and others are adversely affected because of immoral authority and evildoing in high offices. Collectively, we must initiate this objective. Once we can easily point out the existence of Satan's hidden characteristics in others, once we acquire a comprehensive understanding of all the mechanisms and power of Satan, and once we learn how to prohibit his influential capacity of enticing others to follow him that are causing us harm in the world through his tainted political power; only then will we gain realistic control of the nation through rational assessments and understanding of Satan's trickery, from where resolution for correction will then supersede our otherwise ignorance of his ongoing dominance. Other than doing this, we are without current power or intelligent direction to stop him based on the reasonings of mankind. Otherwise, Biblical teachings have already doomed Satan's fate. Meanwhile, we are currently feeling the pain and agony of his injustices here and now while we live. Though God is assured to destroy Satan in due season, should not mean that we should allow Satan to destroy us in the meantime. I am sure that God wants us to do all we can to destroy Satan.

Although religion confronts and addresses this concern, the society as a whole has declined to accept religious belief as trusted standards of facts that should govern what we consider good, evil, right, or wrong ethics and behavior. For this very reason, there is no order, no established understanding, nor any collective or conclusive agreements in the world distinguishing what is definitively right from wrong aside from religion. Personally, I trust religion and Biblical principles, which describes Satan's rise and eventual doom. But for the sake of keeping and respecting the peace of those who have not yet come to grips with accepting religious beliefs or Biblical precepts of reasonings, I am making efforts to discuss this issue as neutral as possible, while leaving room for the expansion of further knowledge, introspection, and potential growth for those who have not yet accepted the concept of spiritual affinity or religion. My wisdom and intellectual discernment is from Good, because I only entertain good thoughts, which produces good concepts, which produces good reasonings, which produces true facts!

If we truly want to overthrow the conflict, violence, and the social and racial unrest that is going on in the nation, we need to discuss the evil dynamic through media outlets and educational platforms, without strict adherence solely to Theological persuasions. This because these media outlets are with the influential capacity to expose those immoral culprits -(evildoers) behind all the controversial issues and problems we are facing as a nation and as a human race! There needs to be an educational awakening through discussions and exchanges of knowledge and ideas about the essence of the spiritual world. It is time to focus on the spiritual dynamics underlying man's mental and emotional conditions based on understood evidence and facts. To assess these basic fundamentals, we don't need religion to merely see evildoers for who they truly are. We don't need religion to make rational assessments, to challenge obvious injustices, or to make productive changes to eliminate apparent evildoers who are positioned to bring corruption and obvious harm upon us. Hitler and others have already shown us the outcome when these types of people are politically empowered.

The truth is that immoral people should be called out for the evildoers they truly are; agents of Satan the devil who could only harm us. This is what we need to do at the end of the day. If this perspective of reasoning is publicly taught, educationally recognized, and then utilized as a basis to identify, to monitor, and to prohibit evildoers from obtaining any political or influential authority over the affairs of humanity; the landscape for peace and democracy will be accomplished. This is what moral people should do for the sake of assuring peace and harmony in all affairs governing the livelihoods of people everywhere. Of course this sounds foreign, because it is. But this is what is needed if we are to find realistic and workable ways to eliminate the evil dynamic from control over our livelihoods. I am certain that some people will call this idealistic pursuit insane. But just like all things in life, everything had a first time beginning. I believe that Satan could be brought under submission here on earth. He has only gained the strength and authority that he has because we have given it to him. Without our participation in his program he has no power. But we must first learn how to study him, how to dissect him, and how to defeat him through the power of the good dynamic, which is the essence God Almighty Himself.

However, by default of our historical inactions and silence to focus on the evil dynamic as we should, the American society has traditionally and substantively hidden and protected Satan and his culprits from accountability for all of the conflict, chaos, and injustice taking place in the nation. Our inactions and silence equals immobility, while immobility equals sitting on your butts doing nothing while the culprit only intensify in his power. We are simply programmed and don't even think about the relevance and power of the evil dynamic from my perspective of reasoning. If we are dissuaded not to think about the evil dynamic for what it truly is, then we are not even inclined to talk about it. And if we are not inclined to talk about it, we are certainly not inclined to study or to educate about it. And if we are not inclined to educate about it, then the masses will forever remain oblivious and ignorant of its true existence.

Its' existence imbeds in the void and lack of understanding that predominates in the mindsets of unscrupulous politicians in whom we must have trust, and hope that they will do the right thing. And this is the problem we are having, because they don't. This is why Satan and the evil dynamic continues to reign in power, while we continue to complain against injustices without realistic resolution, or without even attempting to approach any innovative ways to stop him aside from our customary processes; which is to ignore his evil works and wait on God for vindication. It sounds good, but people are unfairly dying, people are starving, people are homeless, people are sick, people are displaced, and people are needy all over the world right now, while we wait for vindication. I believe that God wants us to take

61

action now and oppose Satan with all the power that He has given to his moral servants, because there is truly a spiritual warfare going on between the good versus the evil forces in the world. It's just that most people don't know or understand this truth yet.

However, we consistently find ourselves in this discontent disposition of vulnerability because the voting populous are oblivious of the evil dynamic's existence from the perspective of reasoning discussed in this book, which is why the evil dynamic under Satan is allowed to subsist and manifest injustices amongst us today with unlimited power, with massive dominance, and with perpetual control over our lives without any censure or realistic liability. This is why those enthralled by Satan and the evil dynamic -(evildoers) are successfully thriving without any realistic resistance or meaningful challenge in political and underhanded economical affairs that are well established in American culture.

No one has stepped up and challenged the supremacy of Satan's rule with real substance, which is either because of fear or because of ignorance. Many of us fear to challenge Satan because of his dangerous tactics, such as murder, deprivation of some right or property, torture, or some other evil and painful infliction as retaliation. If you want to understand firsthand evidence of how Satan works in retaliation against his enemies, simply look at President Donald Trump's political policies and stances. There could be no better example!

The fact is that there is nothing to delimit the power of the evil dynamic in politics, because the voting masses are without any substantive understanding of Satan's supremacy, or how he and his immoral cohorts are adversely impacting the quality of our lives through malevolent and wicked leaders, who are unjustly empowered over the people without realistic challenge, such as President Donald Trump and his comrades.

This is the reason why and how Satan continues to destroy the societal structure and fabric of humanity today. He is discrete and without censure. He is without recognition, for hiding behind his true identity. And he is without any accountability by default of ignorance in American culture, which fails to study the political ways in which he works through the immoral-(evildoers). We simply don't scrutinize or expose Satan or his political cohorts enough, as we should be doing.

The point that I am endeavoring to make is that through our own oblivion, we allow Satan to hide in the midst of antagonism and societal ruin, while we are predisposed to fight among ourselves without rationality or understanding of the intricacies he use to bewilder us through propaganda, trickery, deception, lies, anger, and the daily violence we see going on among us everyday. Through understanding, we can put an end to this depravity, nonetheless.

To see the truth of what is really going on in this regard, you must first come to understand the evil dynamic and its significance to humanity. Only then will you be able to see and understand its relevance to your life, to your destiny, and pertinent to everything that is going on in the world. Otherwise, if you don't acquire a higher level of awareness and understanding of how Satan has deceived the world through the evil dynamic, you will continue to live in the matrix of confusion and mere conformity. Unless you move to a new level of spiritual insight, you will remain a victim of well organized propaganda and lies that are designed to keep the masses intelligently ignorant about the daily mechanisms of Satan and those - (evildoers)- upholding his works of iniquity and depravity in politics, which are literally keeping us divided and confused as a human race.

What I am saying in substance is that we must make Satan and the evil dynamic a priority of awareness through educational study and societal scrutiny, aside from religious teaching alone, of which we have never done collectively as a nation. Understandably, this is because there are too many different religious ideals and too many non-religious people. But despite religion, we must still come to understand that the good and evil dynamic within themselves constitutes the sole premise of human behavior and human ethics nonetheless, which distinguishes right from wrong everywhere in life. As you should realize at this point, religions merely confirms this truth. The analogies that I am expressing here is the educational curriculum and understanding that should have been, but never was. As a consequence of not considering or seeing the evil dynamic from my perspective of reasoning, we are left with what we currently see in America and abroad; an evil world without understanding, without universal order, and a world that is without control over the evil dynamic that is otherwise destroying peaceful human relations all over the earth.

As already exemplified in prior discussion, nothing good will ever result from anything that is evil or bad, which is why the bad and evil element is definitively wrong in all of its workings. The truth is that evil is wrong because it helps no one or nothing.

It is only grounded in harm, pain, conflict, and premature death. Meanwhile, the preeminence of God, good works, peace, love, and good things are the only things that are worthy in this life. Why? Because only good things can help us. And we all need help, which only comes from God alone! This is why the good element alone is definitively right and righteous as universal law amongst all of humanity. No matter what religion anyone may embrace, at the end of the day all religions will lead to this one and only conclusion!

For this reason, it makes good sense that it should not take just religion alone to instill this simple understanding, as has become customary practice in America and in other cultures. And truthfully, even religious teachings within themselves today fail to instill this basic understanding without confusion, even when taught from the most simplest and direct method of Biblical analysis. When it is all broken down to its most simplistic terms of understanding, religion merely educates that there are two dynamics that constitutes mankind's entire existence, his fate, and his destiny now and in the after life relative to his free will to choose between the good and the evil courses of life.

Religion teaches that the good dynamic promises eternal bliss, while the bad dynamic promises eternal torment. From the

Christian angle of reasoning, these understandings are instilled through stories, illustrations, and parables in the Bible to enforce our faith and trust in the divine.

Metaphorically, my approach to the evil dynamic, as expressed within these pages, addresses the relevance of Satan, and how he uses the evil dynamic to work to his advantage averse to others who are otherwise destined for harm by following his course of life in any capacity. This is actually the primary point that Pastors are endeavoring to teach to its parishioners in churches all around the world at the end of the day. Church is merely about understanding the good from the evil, and distinguishing what is right from wrong relative to these two principles. I must reemphasize that whether one believes in God or not, the truth is that nothing good could ever harm you, while nothing bad could ever help you or anyone else anywhere on earth, which again, is because of the evil dynamic's innate harm and destructive nature. The truth is that Satan and all evildoing is ugly, and God does not like any evil or ugly thing,

I am endeavoring to explain to those who may not know, that every disorder and bad thing going on in this world about anything whatsoever, is because of some evil act perpetrated by some evil person/s; all influenced in one way or another by the demonic forces of Satan and the evil dynamic, which is his weapon of mass destruction. I am endeavoring to enforce the understanding that despite any religious ideal, the dynamics of good and evil are the highest spiritual principles that all of mankind must deal with in the world, whether we like it or not. I am endeavoring to instill an understanding that these two dynamics exist within a classification all alone, from which all ethics, principles, and rationalities of life are predicated upon.

I am merely advocating that religion merely confirms that one dynamic will help you, (Good), while the other dynamic, (Evil/bad), will harm you. And since no one wants to be harmed anyplace on earth, religion attempts to have us to distinguish between good and evil, in efforts to avoid only the the evil, from which all harm and pain originates under the forces of Satan the devil who we all dread. Meanwhile, it is apparent and common practice behavior that we are all endeavoring to embrace help and love under the forces of God, because only God provides to us those good things, which are the only things that keeps us all alive and happy on earth.

I am endeavoring to edify an understanding that regardless if you believe in any specific religion or not, the good and evil dynamics exist, and that religion merely confirms their existence, confirms their relativity to man's existence, confirms their impact in our reasonings and behaviors relative to their existence, and confirms man's destined fate in retrospect to his free will to choose the good or evil course of life relative to each dynamic's distinctive nature and existence. I am endeavoring to enforce an understanding that these truths are not just mere theories, presumptions, speculations, or conjectures without significance to our daily livelihoods, as many immoral people would mislead us to believe.

If you choose only the good course of life by only doing good works by helping others in some way, you are a moral and righteous person because you are doing the works of God at the end of the day. If you choose the evil course of life by routinely engaging in evil, bad, or harmful activities, you are immoral and wrong, regardless of whatever your reasonings are. The proof; the evil dynamic will only harm others, while the good dynamic will only help others. The logic is that no one wants to be harmed anywhere on earth, which makes harm definitively wrong; while everyone wants to be helped everywhere in existence, of which only good things are capable of helping us; which makes helping others definitively right.

The Help or Harm Analysis

For all reasons stated herein above, I advocate that Congress should establish what I term a Help or Harm Analysis, which is a means to weed out the good from the evil segments seeking political and other relevant offices where peoples lives, freedom, and quality of livelihoods are at stake. A help or harm analysis will be a system of scrutiny that will allow Congress to evaluate any ethic, any deed, any policy, any law, any procedure, any act, or any behavior of any political candidate, leader, or others entrusted with political power in the world, as a means to identify moral versus the immoral segments on account of the harm or help each propose under their political agendas and perspectives.

This system of scrutiny is what is needed in the world, but is unfortunately missing in our political reasonings under Constitutional standards, which is due to a separation of powers between the Church and the State, of which I suspect was more than likely orchestrated somehow by the influence of Satan at one point of time in our history, who simply cannot afford to have only the good dynamic dominate the fate of the nation. In doing this, Satan has placed himself on the same ethical level as God, relative to the fundaments of the United States Constitutional provisions under the Equal Protection, First

Amendment, and Equal Rights clauses. Ask yourself, why should Satan have any rights at all, when we already understand and clearly know that his only objective is to bring harm upon us? How much sense does that really make?

But the truth is that Satan has rights, which is the number one problem. It's like giving a gun to an angry, mean spirited, violent, crazed, and chronic killer that has already murdered over 100 people, but who has never been disciplined in his life, yet released without ever being charged to roam free and at the exposure of his most worst hated enemies, but yet expected not to shoot anyone because he has equal rights to possess a gun. We already know his nature, we already know his background, we already know his capabilities, we already know how dangerous he is; and yet because he has equal rights, we still put a weapon in hands and expect for him follow the rules.

How unrealistic is that? It is just as realistic as giving Satan Equal Rights under the United States Constitution, knowing full well that no righteousness is found in him, but yet expecting him to do the right thing. This is why we need to look further into whether or not one's nature is harmful to us before consenting, electing, or before voting any person into political office at any level of government. The harmful should not even be allowed to be placed on the ballot in the first place. And the only way to assure that he or she is not allowed to do so, is to utilize a Help or Harm Analysis to ascertain the true nature of one's character on account of his or her's sentiments, values, opinions, background, ideals, beliefs, temperamental attitude, and mental acuity. An analysis of these factors will enable us to pinpoint who we are actually dealing with. It will allow us to decipher the good versus the bad qualities in one's true character, which will amount to being a moral or an immoral person. This is a realistic and practicable method that is assured to work effectively by which to make such determination, provided that we adhere to these simple principles.

If we seriously want peace, harmony, and freedom from the potential harm posed by evildoers who are gone wild; then this specific concept of knowledge and understanding should be normalized in American education, as well as in other cultures, provided we are to delimit the power and influence of Satan. In this modern day history, there should be new standards of education focusing on the evil dynamic based on the help or harm analysis's to decipher out, to scrutinize, and by which to delimit the power, influence, and control of satanic people and influential forces of the evil dynamic from operating within all political spheres, which substantively governs the livelihoods and destiny of people all over the earth.

The truth is that we only need God through Jesus Christ, or at the least to conform to the concept and principles of God, if peace is truly the objective at the end of the day, regardless of any religious indoctrination by and within itself. And please respect, that I am by no means speaking against God, against spirituality, or against the Christian doctrine under the New Testament of Jesus. But at the end of the day, we must first deal with the only reality we all know, and the only reality that we have experienced. And we must also deal with the only reality that we are currently experiencing in our lives right now. And right now, Satan, immorality, and evildoers are dominating the livelihoods of the masses all around the world through political tyranny, and they are doing so without any true challenge or prevention to cease and desist anytime soon.

But if we were to institute a Help or Harm Analysis as a basis to scrutinize and decipher this evil element out, we could realistically restore peaceful human relations, or rightfully resort to spiritual warfare that will be led by no other than God Himself. If God is for us, no other weapon formed against us will ever prevail. Some of us believe this, but there are millions of others who don't, for lack of faith.

The Attributes of Moral Versus Immoral People

I think that it is important to have a distinctive understanding of the characteristics that distinguishes moral people from immoral people. This is because there are too many immoral people running around in the world who fight and complain against injustices of one kind or another, not actually realizing that they themselves are evil, and are no better than those against whom they complain. Because there are no specific guidelines or established set of principles that identifies or deem the good or evil nature of people's integrity from a neutral, fair, and unbiased perspective; the best way to make these determinations is to examine the innate mental and psychological faculties underlying the thinking, beliefs, reasonings, values, and the integrity of people. This will allow us to distinguish one's moral or immoral temperament based on their mental attitudes and levels of tolerance. The Bible encourages us to be Christ-like, which means that we should be humble, understanding, kind, and gentle natured people. Even though some of the worst criminals are with the capacity to display these same Godly characteristics at times; one's true character is truly tested when put under pressure. It is tested when things are unjustifiably done to us, when things unfairly happens to us, or when unfavorable things happens to us to such an extent that we either humble ourselves and accept the situation with grace, or we succumb to anger, violence, and aggression; seeking to avenge injustice by our own means. When we succumb to anger, rage, and violence, and go on a rampage seeking our own justice, we have failed the test! But this does not mean that we are incapable of restoring our dignity in the sight of God by later repenting. Such behavior will remain a sinful and accountable act until it is covered through one's repentance and God's forgiveness.

The attributes of God is morality, love, peace, joy, happiness, forgiveness, help, and compassion. These are the attributes of moral people. Moral people are Godly, loving, compassionate, understanding, considerate, kind, and helpful to others. This is why the concept of God is definitively right, regardless of any specific religion. Right from wrong ethics are predicated on the basis of whether people are helped or harmed at the end of the day. Not too many people truly understand this truth. No moral person anywhere will hurt others for no apparent reason, aside from in self-defense of impending harm, or because of some threat to his or her safety by an immoral or evil element.

Help only comes from God and by good things alone, while harm only comes from Satan and bad things alone. Whether anyone is harmed in any capacity by another, is proof standing all alone that such harm is the definitive work of an immoral person whose spirit is ruled by Satan the devil, which makes that person bad and definitively wrong, regardless of the situation. This is why wrongdoing is called sin!

The attributes of an immoral person are hatred, anger, lying, envy, jealousy, and violence, which leads to countless conflicting circumstances that causes chaos and untimely death. Anyone ascribing to these characteristics are being ruled by Satan and the evil dynamic, whether they know it or not. These are the attributes dominated by immoral people who may not see themselves for the immoral people they truly are in nature. You don't have to know or understand that you are immoral; your nature, attitude, and psychological disposition speaks for itself. You are all alone in a class all by yourself based on you being you. You cannot go outside of yourself and be anyone different than who you actually are.

You cannot perceive yourself from the same lens from which the external world sees you, judges you, condemns you, or embraces you. There are things about you that no one is going to tell you about what they truly see and feel about you; no more than there are things that you perceive about others that you would dare to tell them. But at the end of the day, people are either moral or immoral, with the capacity to be swayed either way in life, depending on whether one chooses to follow Satan or follow God's course of life.

For the most part, no one thinks that anything is wrong with them, despite how terrible of a person he or she may be in our own eyes. The Bible says that God looks at the heart of people. That is where the real you lies, regardless of the facades of falsehoods that are buried beneath the shield of deceptions we each carry. The truth is that people simply don't rationalize against themselves because they feel they already know who they are.

In our own minds we justify every single bad thing that we have ever done, and eventually convince ourselves that it was really not that bad after all. The Bible says that everyone is right in his or her own eyes, but God weighs the heart. Those things that are deeply imbedded in your heart is who you truly are at the end of the day. The ugly little secrets that you are hiding are not hidden at all because God sees them. Making attempts to hide those demons without repentance is sinful and immoral behavior. It is immoral because you are attempting to conceal the truth of knowing wrongdoing without asking for forgiveness, which makes you someone other than people presume you to be. At the end of the day, this is deception. It means you are living a lie. It means that people of this nature are untrustworthy, cunning, deceptive, and immoral.

Immoral people are also vengeful, mean-spirited, wicked, inconsiderate, and very unkind. Immoral people are prone to bring harm, sadness, or some adverse condition upon others without regard for love, compassion, or forgiveness. There are many people who are this way who will stand on the front line and fight against injustices going on somewhere, while they themselves may have stolen something a few minutes ago, or may have lied someone, or may have cheated someone, or maybe have cursed someone out for some reason, or maybe became violent and got into a fight and beat up someone, or maybe they drink and use excessive profanity, or maybe engage in substance abuse, or maybe indulge in two-faced chattering behind the backs of friends, or may have commit adultery, or may have murdered someone, or may have commit race discrimination, or may have committed other immoral acts. Despite that these people are practicing immoral behaviors themselves, most of these same people are protesting all over the world against the works of Satan. Yet, these are clearly Satan's people themselves, because one would have to be immoral to do any of these sinful things.

This is how you should determine the immoral people who is of Satan, versus the moral people who is of God. Neither is perfect, nonetheless, but God favors the just. People of Satan tend to bring some facet of harm upon us; while people of God only brings help to us in some manner. These mere principles are what truly defines the basis of who is moral from immoral, and what is definitively right from wrong, of which most people have not yet figured out, regardless of any specific religion. All religions are merely confirmations to this one and only principle. It is very important to understand this!

President Donald Trump

Now that we have a clear conception of the evil dynamic and its attributing characteristics, let us honestly examine the disposition of today's political leader, President Donald Trump. And this is not merely to condemn, to degrade, or to belittle Trump, but to demonstrate a living reality that is inescapable of the truth; given all of the irrefutable evidence, facts, and Biblical analysis's, which is all we have. Given all of this proof, what else are we to do?

If you have already read the chapters preceding this discussion, I am confident that by now you already know the moral or immoral status of President Trump at this point of discussion. But for the sake of being realistic and to reinforce all said herein-above, this analysis must be told for the sake of acquiring a clear understanding, and for the sake of justice through knowledge for those who may need to truly grasp the logistics underlying this discussion as it relates to Trump.

For example, today in America, President Donald Trump demonstrates the clearest example ever to convince us that he is the actual son of Satan the devil from the evil dynamic who is responsible for every human disorder on earth. There is no other person in today's time, other than Putin, that displays the kind of wicked and evil conduct that is clearly indicative of Satan and the evil dynamic, than Trump by far. This is irrefutably confirmed according to Biblical teaching itself. There is no other book in existence that provides mankind with the most accurate understanding of good and evil than the Holy Bible, of which Trump himself has asserted is his favorite book. Every concerned person should come to understand the below truth for the indisputable principles that it establishes. Please read (Proverbs) 29:2, that says ***"When the righteous are in authority, the people rejoice: <u>but when the wicked beareth rule, the people mourn.</u>"*** This is quoted from Trump's favorite book!

What is this saying to us? This is implying that when moral - (Righteous) people are in authority, people are happy, people are content, and people are not stressing or depressed under moral leadership. This is substantively saying that people are satisfied with the way things are going when moral people bear rule because there is no mourning. This is because moral people are righteous people who bring help to us. They show love to us. They show compassion for us. They create peace amongst us. These are the characteristics of the righteous people amongst us in the world. These are Godly people because they are loving, compassionate, kind, helpful, giving, and understanding people.

They are not perfect people; but they are kind and fair people who make concessions to help those who they represent. They show compassion for the less fortunate. They cause people to rejoice, despite they have faults too, because no one is perfect. Well, except for Donald Trump, as he will never admit that he has any flaws whatsoever!

On the other hand, the Bible is also saying in this verse that *when the wicked is in authority, the people mourn*; meaning that the people complain, groan, protest, and are not happy. This precept is implying that the people are revolting because of a wicked ruler that somehow poses some facet of discomfort or harm to them. It is substantively saying that the people are not at peace under his Presidency -(Rule). In other words, it implies that when the wicked -(Unrighteous) is in authority, there is uproar, protest, and societal unrest! Look around; not only in America, but all over the world people are mourning under Donald Trump's authority. If not already, this should awaken you!

The Bible is substantively saying here that Satan is now running America. It is saying that the wicked is in power. How is this confirmed? Because millions of people are mourning because of Trumps' evil stances. Or, could it be that the Bible is lying? His stances have resulted in mass deprivations, in vengeance against those he dislikes instead of forgiveness, have resulted in division amongst the people on account of political difference, have resulted in division amongst people on account of race, and have resulted to the implementation of antagonistic policies that were devised from his clear and immoral state of anger and relentless hatred. Biblical precepts clearly confirms that Trump is evil, and no more evidence is needed other than the fact that people are mourning all over the nation because of his leadership. What is the difference between wickedness and evil? A wicked person is someone who lives in opposition to God's laws and righteousness, often characterized by rejection of God's commandments and pursuit of sinful desires. These are Satan's characteristics, who is the king of the evil dynamic, as clearly reflected in every element of Trump's behavior, personality, and character.

I am only making this point to confirm that Trump's behavior is a manifestation of Satan the devil and the evil dynamic, as already discussed at length! This is also to confirm that he is definitively wrong in all that he does. This also confirms that each and every single person who supports or follows him are all evil and wrong in all they think and do as well. This truth confirms that all of his followers are immoral and is of Satan the devil as well. This is also to confirm that none of his followers are of God because they don't do good works on behalf of all the people. If they did, the people would be not mourning under their leadership in concert with Donald Trump. The Bible clearly exposed these truths!

Despite this truth, Trump and his fallen angels profess to be God-loving Christians. I mean, really, come on! Think about that for a moment, while mentally brewing over all that has already been said and discussed at length about Satan, about the evil dynamic, about the good dynamic, about the moral, about the immoral, and all that has already been said about the distinctive characteristics that makes a person morally right from immorally wrong, which is based on whether people are helped or harmed relative to a leader's political objectives, actions, and/or aspirations.

Only a fool would go along with the absurd allegation that Trump and his angels are people of God, or that they serve the doctrines of Jesus to any extent whatsoever. In fact, they have all sinned and should face retribution by God for simply making such a ridiculous protestation of blasphemy that they are Christians, when in fact they are haters who only promotes violence, hatred, anger, division, race discrimination, economic deprivation, job discrimination, education discrimination, health discrimination, and societal unrest, among many other evils. Yet,

85

these are people who proclaim to be Godly people who are running the nation.

None of these above assertions are merely speculative, nor could be rationally disputed by anyone. The world bear witness to the actual evidence of their evildoings nearly 24 hours a day. Just the mere fact that Trump and the Republican Regime have deemed themselves Christians should be shocking to the conscience of any sane, moral, or reasonable person. If they were true Christians, wouldn't they show love, compassion, kindness, and understanding of the feelings and concerns of others? Would not they show characteristics of Jesus in their reasonings, since they claim to be Christians? Wouldn't they help the less fortunate? Wouldn't they be forgiving of others for the countless allegations they claim that others have done wrong to them, instead of doing all they can to seek their own vengeance contrary to the Bible's instructions that vengeance belongs to God, which is their favorite book?

They possess none of these moral characteristics. Instead, Trump is mean spirited, always angry about something, antagonistic, name calling, vengeful, and self-centered; which is called narcissistic. The entire nation witness these characteristics in Donald Trump and in nearly all of his followers around the clock. He could never hide who he truly is. The people clearly see, understand, and know exactly who he is. Yet, this president is full of himself without any consideration for the fact that he is under perpetual scrutiny by the whole world for who he really is. This is not to judge him; but to merely respect an observation of facts exposing who he has presented himself to be. He himself has proven to be an evil person!

The Danger of American Journalism & Trump

Think about it; if all of Trump supporters are clearly not of God, then we need to ask ourselves why are news journalists and national media net works even projecting upon their concerns, high-lighting their propositions, their ideals, their opinions, their complaints, or even broadcasting the perspectives of these immoral people? Why are they treating their agendas as meritorious matters that are worthy of public interest and concern, which only provides an undeserved platform in support of Satan, which only allows his perpetual evildoing to persist through his immoral -(evildoers) servants?

We truly need to ask ourselves, why are the concerns and agendas of the immoral segment even relevant to journalists in the first place, seeing they clearly mean no good and have no good intentions to sincerely help the people who they serve? Why are the concerns and agendas of these immoral people treated as significant and normal matters of interest, when they are not even worthy to be discussed, given the understandable nature of who they really are?

It is already apparent that the immoral have no worthy causes. Yet, news journalists listen to these ridiculous people, and then project their immaterial perspectives upon the minds of the masses nonetheless. What this does is keep Satan in the game. It gives him the privilege of staying in the game to throw dirt in a fight that he has long lost without censure or liability as it already stands. Yet, the media assists in allowing him to still retain rights and rank as a champion who has long lost his crown. In fact, he has never even had a crown in the first place. It is only because of the media that he is even still around because they keep focusing on him and blowing up his significance by reporting every word he says, everything he does, and every act that he makes, when in fact none of it is anything of real substance. The media creates the substance of Trump, and shoves it down the throats of the people, to the point where millions of gullible, uneducated, naive, lost, and confused people fall for the hype who collectively paint him as a hero, when in fact he is a demon.

It is unfortunate that the media has given Satan a platform, has given him respect, and has given him an audience of which he can further entice, manipulate, and influence support, by which he could eventually manifest his harmful objectives against us all in the guise of a lie that his draconian policies are what the people asked for because they allegedly voted him in office. Too often common citizens are not aware of or concerned about the treacherous power of the media and journalists who are with the influential capacity to shape, control, and manifest societal thought, behavior, and perspectives. Although there are many journalists whom I admire, I still cannot surpass the fact that they too have resorted to empower Trump by too often giving him an undeserved platform.

Rationalizing from a moral perspective of reasoning, Satan does not deserve and should not have such respect and persuasive capacity over the mindset of the masses through news journalism, but he does. Yet, it is apparent that American journalists do not see it this way. The only realistic alternative to reach in this regard, is to conclude that many of the journalists themselves are of the same immoral nature as Satan. Or perhaps they don't realize, or don't understand, or don't know, or don't care, or are simply carrying out protocol of news reporting and issues of discussion as demanded by immoral superiors and bosses in high offices who are of Satan themselves. It could also be because of news ratings. It is true that Trump is a very controversial figure who people are now waiting to hear about.

The fact of the matter is that the methodology of journalism in America is the true problem to the nation's unrest to a very relevant extent, and it seems as if the right people has figured it out! It is a proven fact that the media has the capacity to captivate, to influence, to hold, and to sway both the attention and behavior of the masses; given its undeniable power of persuasion through both propaganda and real facts, of which they could manipulate truth either way! At the end of the day, it is the media that controls the pervasive behavior of the people, which is by default of controlling perception and thought at the behest of wealthy and immoral elites who are speciously pulling strings of favoritism behind closed doors.

When the media allows deception and lies to go rampant and unfettered, despite being able to dispel such falsehoods; it substantively supports and sustains such lies. In doing this, it enters into agreement with Satan to keep the wool pulled over the peoples' eyes. Its gives credence, power, and influence to the evildoer, and unfairly shields the actual culprits from scrutiny, from retribution, from detection, and from public accountability. This truth demonstrates the dangerous power of the media when controlled by the immoral elite. This is how Satan continues to sustain in American politics, and is how it has empowered Trump to sustain political dominance.

If Trump was not evil, then there would be no massive mourning of the citizens, there would be no massive protests, there would be no incentive for war, there would be no motivation for racial division, there would be no incentives to fight amongst each other, there would be no massive societal unrest, and there would be no mass chaos going on all over the world under his presidency. The media could focus upon these issues and make these issues priorities and concerns if they wanted to. The media could talk about the evil dynamic, Satan, and Trump's propensity for evildoing as evidenced by his behavior, his policies, and by his overall immoral nature. These things are not below the threshold of journalistic concerns, but are yet suppressed in favor of issues that deviates from these truths, and thus misleading the masses away from pertinent and meritorious issues of the utmost importance to their life, liberty, and livelihoods.

The truth is that it is the evildoing itself that is imbedded in Trump's rationale and thinking, as orchestrated under the influence of Satan and the evil dynamic, which is induces and promotes the chaos we see in the world. Chaos is what compels man to divide, to fight against himself, and is what makes us destroy each other. Chaos is caused by anger, and anger begets violence. Both anger and violence are attributes of the evil dynamic under the influential power of Satan. And evildoing itself is Satan's very essence and means to challenge the sovereignty of God and all of His good attributes, of which God devised for the peace and harmony of humanity. The media refuse to disseminate this true line of reasoning to the masses, thereby allowing Satan to thrive without realistic opposition against the evil dynamic.

Yet, as already expressed; these two relevant dynamics – (*Good & Evil*), their spiritual attributes, and their metaphysical relevance to humanity are not routinely nor unilaterally enforced within the thinking of the masses outside of religious indoctrination, as they should be. Moreover, these two dynamics are not a matter of public awareness through educational tutoring, of which they should be, but are buried in oblivion and in the darkness of ignorance, which is partially due to the American journalists who refused to expose the evil dynamic through their platforms of national discussions.

Lack of education explaining this very principle to the masses aside from religious indoctrination, is what is missing in human relations, and is why violence and conflict continues to destroy the fabric of human and race relations everywhere. National media net works are very vital to the American perspective, and when it fails to disclose or expose evildoers for who they truly are, it becomes part of the problem and not the solution. It becomes the culprit itself, because its inactions shows conspiratorial evidence to conceal plain and obvious injustices of which it alone has the power to expose, which has an adverse effect on the nation when they fail to do so.

Why The Bible Should Be Perceived From A Metaphysical Perspective of Reasoning

Of course I have periodically talked about the Bible in several references throughout preceding discussions, but never actually got down to the bare meat and potatoes of this concern. This is important because the Bible is the most controversial book ever written, and is the most supreme doctrine that unravels questions, speculations, opinions, conjectures, viewpoints, and philosophical perspectives unlike any other book written anywhere on the earth. Yet, it still remains the most puzzling book as well because not everyone can understand or interpret its fundamental essence with absolute certainty aside from mere belief. And this is not to deny or to minimize the significance of the Bible or its' precepts.

But because there is so much world confusion, conflicting opinions, and varying religious denominations deriving from the Bible because of disagreements in meanings and questionable interpretations; there is a need to shift from our delimited perspectives of the Bible and religion itself, and start looking at life from a more metaphysical angle of reasoning relative to the principles underlying religion as a whole. Why? Because over half of alleged believers are fooling themselves, and making themselves look like foolish hypocrites by professing to believe in the Bible, when deep down inside they know they don't believe in anything. Most people claim they believe in the Bible and God merely because of family upbringing, peer pressure, people pleasing, and wanting to belong and to be a part of something. Others go along for the ride just because they simply want to be accepted and go along with the flow; knowing deep down inside they have no true faith.

But, it should not have to be this way. It is okay not to believe. It is okay to be skeptical. It is okay to admit your apprehensions about God and the Bible. There are many justifiable reasons why people don't believe in the Bible. But that does not mean that the Bible is not true. It merely means that some people don't understand it. Some people don't get it, and some people will never get it. There are thousands of things written in the Bible that sounds ridiculous to me, but I am wise enough to know that whether they are true or not, to stay focused on the primary objective of the Bible without getting sideswiped by its specificities; meaning by relying on every specific word written in the Book as the absolute truth. This is because specificities could be very misleading because each specific word written in the Bible was not the only one and specific word in its original meaning, context, or connotative expression. It only takes the misunderstanding, the misinterpretation, the misconception, or the misperception of just one single word to throw off a person's entire understanding of the Bible when reading it based on its specific words. This is specially important when considering so many different versions and translations of the Bible.

All words written in the Bible were translated from various other languages by various other men who had various other verbiages and understandings in their contextual expressions and view points; all which were inconsistent with what each other probably would have conveyed in meaning on the same topics as discussed and written in the Bible. No two people use the same exact set of words to explain themselves, to talk about a matter, or to discuss a matter, because there are varying words with the same meaning. Everyone explains themselves according to each's education, knowledge, and understanding, which includes words. Some people have an expansive comprehension consisting of thousands of words; while others live an entire lifetime with only 50 words in his or her vocabulary.

The person with only an understanding of 50 words in his vocabulary will not express a story as clear and vivid as one with thousands of words in his or her vocabulary. Despite that both may experience the same event, once writing about the event to explain to others what happened at the event; at the end of the day, you are going to get two different versions about what happened at the same event. And somewhere down the line those stories will be witnessed by others. The wise will understand that both stories are true because the wise looks beyond the stories and focus on the essence of the event that took place relative to the story. The wise understand that there is more than one way to perceive the same truth regardless of who tells the story.

But there are too many people in life who are very specific, who takes every literal word and break that single word down to its' minute definition in efforts to prove a point, when it's not even about that one word all the while. What this does is create conflict, confusion, and division. And this happens all the time with many Pastors and Religious freaks. They get so caught up using up valuable energy getting into the specificity of this or that word, until they lose sight of the most important principle of what the Bible is actually conveying in the context of the story.

The context is the substantive nature of what the story is saying beyond the words. The words are merely trying to make you understand the context of the story. But if you look only for the context, the words are insignificant because the context focuses on the metaphysical nature behind the words and the story. In other words, the context is the overall scope and meaning of the Bible, which is to bring you into submission to the good dynamic ruled by God, and to draw you away from the evil dynamic, ruled by Satan the devil. At the end of the day, that is the contextual foundation of the Bible. But it provides stories, examples, and parables in efforts to instill this contextual understanding to discipline the parishioners, with Jesus being the Supreme model who walked upon the earth without sin. The rest is faith, which is the cornerstone of all possibilities. But if we focus on the specificities of every single word in the Bible in efforts to understand its' contextual meaning; somewhere along the way people get lost, confused, and in many cases walk away and don't even try get the point because of the complexities and lack of understanding of specific words and their overall meaning. Pastors are even guilty of this themselves.

Let's say that I walking down the streets, and I notice a gentleman passing by and decide to speak to him by saying, "Hello brother. How are you doing?" Let's say at the same time, a young lady was close enough to witness and hear my greetings to him. Let's say that at some time later, the young lady who witnessed me greeting the man, was into a conversation with a friend. And as they were talking, I drove past them and waived to them. The lady who witnessed me greet the gentleman that was walking by, asks her friend if she knows me. The friend says, "Oh, yeah I know him. We went to school together." She then asks, why, do you know him? And she then says, "No, but I know he has a brother." And the friend says, "I know his entire family, and he doesn't have any brothers." But the young lady insists that she knows what she is talking about because she witnessed and heard for herself that I called the man that walked pass my brother.

At the end of the day, brother means brother, right? But that was merely my way of expressing myself, just as people have been doing since the dawn of time. In order for everyone to speak the same specific words when expressing themselves, they would have to learn the same language at the same time, think exactly the same way, have the same habits, the same family rearing, the same educational and spiritual backgrounds, and think exactly alike with the same vocabulary expression in their dialects and verbiages. And even then, each is not going to tell the same story using the same set of specific words, despite having the same experience about a matter.

One may say that it was cold outside during some fight between two people, while another might say that it was a cool night during the fight. While another writing about the same fight, might say that it was a freezing night. How do you determine what is the truth? By the time a person figures out the truth, the entire essence, metaphysical nature, and context of the story gets lost without any understanding at all. This is because they are still trying to figure out what kind of night it was during the fight, while the fight was the central issue to focus on. And because there is so much trouble, uncertainty, and conflicting accounts about how the weather was, about who said who said what, and what is or not true; soon people will lose faith and trust if the fight ever even happened. But what all witnesses did have in common, is the fact that there was a fight, regardless of the weather that night. The fight was the central concern and principle, no less than the metaphysics of the Bible is that it is designed to make us understand that there are good and evil dynamics that will either help or harm you, and it is your job to conform to the good dynamic by following the principles of Jesus and not Satan.

All of the underlying specifics relative to trying to make you understand this fact about the Bible will only slow down your overall progress because of its questionable differences, expressions, conflicting accounts, and other variances that puts to question its authenticity as facts and God's divine word. Let's not focus on if the weather was cold, cool or freezing during the fight; let's focus on the fact that there was a fight. Let's not focus on every specific word in the Bible, or the specificity of the Bible; let's look at its' metaphysical meaning and intent of expression for what it is saying in substance. In substance it is saying not to walk in the way of evil because you will be punished. That is what the stories, parables, and examples are conclusively saying in the Bible at the end of the day, and this is the only understanding you should get from it after all is said and done. It teaches that Jesus established the perfect example regarding how we should live, and served as the perfect model of which we should conform in efforts to reach eternal salvation. Otherwise, why should it take so much bickering, doubt due to lack of understanding a simple word or two in meaning, dialect, or interpretation; when the Bible's fundamental nature is what it is?

This angle of reasoning is not to deny or dispute the fundaments of Christianity or any other religious denomination. But this rationale of reasoning is to look outside of a religion's direct verbiage in its specific expression of words, and instead look at religion's overall context and fundamental meaning relative to its' overall essence. This is the only objective on this specific issue of the Bible. I trust in the Bible, but I question some of its logics because I know for certain that it was not all of God's people who wrote the Bible. I say this because there is a section of the Bible that says slave be subservient to your masters. There is no way under the sun that anyone is going to make me believe that God wrote those words. Those words were written by white slave owners, who wanted to assure the obedience and subserviency of Black slaves. Just that mere fact alone, put hesitation in my spirit and intellectual capacity of reasoning relative to the Bible. Even the Holy Spirit itself nudged my conscience and even the DNA of my mental acuity and told me that it is a no good for nothing lie. For that reason, I kind of move through the precepts of the Bible with caution, yet still respecting its fundaments and overall metaphysics relative to Satan, and the good and evil dynamics governing the behavior of mankind on earth.

The problem is that too many people are caught up into religious specificity, which causes too many intelligent minds to overlook the simplicity and metaphysical understanding of good versus evil attributes, which should otherwise be perceived and exemplified as paradigms of justice versus injustices, by which to instill knowledge and understanding to the world about how the essence of those two dynamics - (good & evil) - affects every element of man's right or wrong, or moral versus immoral behavior, regardless of religion. And this is to take nothing away from Biblical teachings in its metaphysical meaning or its' fundamental principle.

So, to reiterate this perspective from another set of words, the truth is that the entire Bible and Biblical precepts rests on these two distinctive factors at the end of the day; with the good dynamic being superior to the evil dynamic. The metaphysical science is that one dynamic will help us, while the other dynamic will harm us. Since no one embraces harm, which is manifested from the evil dynamic; the only detrimental dynamic, the evil dynamic is definitively wrong. But the good dynamic, in representation of God, is what everyone wants and needs in his or her life, which is why it is definitively right.

And once again; conforming to the evil dynamic is definitively wrong because of its' innate harm that no one welcomes into his or her life anywhere on earth. These are actual living principles (good & evil) that has a negative or positive effect in the livelihoods of humanity everywhere. Metaphysically, all religions are attempting to make this clear by one means or another through stories, examples, and spiritual principles underlying good versus evil ethics. Ignoring this most fundamental truth merely sets us up for confusion, misunderstanding, and misdirection in our ethics and reasonings in life, even in light of religious teachings.

Reasoning from the Christian perspective, the Bible provide stories and examples to exemplify to us that all who chose the evil dynamic through his or her free will, met with failure, destruction, and untimely death; while all who chose the good dynamic under the authority and preeminence of God, eventually met with happiness, joy, and eternal bliss by one means another. If we read Biblical scripture in minute detail, and rely on every single word with specificity in relation to our specific understanding, it is possible to lose sight of the overall and most important objective of its' teachings at the end of the day. This is why the most wise teachers of Biblical scriptures utilizes the Concordat, which interchanges, breaks down, and redefine various words in root meanings, dialects, and languages according to different times periods recorded by different generations and people who recorded events that took place over the course of history.

In other words, the Bible was written thousands of years ago and translated and re-translated by different people, who spoke different languages, which had different meanings in both dialects and connotative understandings. So, what I am saying in this conversation is why not just look at its' metaphysical nature and meaning of the Bible in its' totality? Again, in its' totality the Bible is saying that the only right way of life is to do all good works, strive for all good things, and live only for those things that are good because only good works and good things will help you, while all evil works and all bad things will harm you.

The Bible is substantively saying that if you don't want eternal harm and pain in your life, stay way from Satan, away from immoral people, and away from evil characteristics, which are called sins. In its precepts the Bible set standards, rules, and examples for us to do these things, with Jesus as the prime example of perfection of whom we should model after.

This is what religion is all about at the end of the day. But not too often is it broken down so that ordinary people could understand its' metaphysical meaning without confusion over every minute detail of Biblical verbiage, and its specificity of every single word. It only takes the misunderstanding of one word, sentence, or meaning to confuse people about the whole essence of what the Bible is substantively saying.

This is why there are so many different religious denominations, while there is only one metaphysical principle that equally governs all religious ideals: which is a challenge of right from wrong relative to distinctions of the good and evil dynamic, of which are in symbolization of God and Satan. See, race has nothing to do with these principles at the end of the day, because anyone is capable of possessing either characteristic through his or her free will that is equally given to all human beings, regardless of anyone's race.

What it all boils down to at the end of the day, is that God and the essence of his good attributes supersedes all else in the world, because it is only by good things why mankind subsist on earth in the first place. And it is only because of the bad things, why he cannot sustain his life on earth. This is why we all need God, regardless of race or religion, because God and the word good are synonymous to each other, and are the only words keeping us all alive.

Anger

When you think about this word, you see violence, someone frowning, someone fighting, someone hurting another, someone arguing with another, someone in fury, someone in rage, someone using profanity, someone killing another, someone thinking about or contemplating on harming someone in some way. You see, there is entirely nothing good whatsoever that anger could ever produce under any circumstance. Entirely nothing good could ever come from this state! Yet, think about all of the angry political leaders and others who support them that are out there in the society, who actually have a beef on their shoulders about one thing or another, and who feel that they should take grievous matters into their own hands. These are very dangerous people, because anger is Satan's number one mechanism of destruction, while society treat anger as an ordinary walk in the park on a sunny day. This is a very serious issue!

In order for a person to be angry, it means that he or she is harboring evil thoughts, violent thoughts, negative thoughts, or destructive thoughts; all belonging to the evil dynamics of Satan. The truth is that nothing good or productive could ever result from any of these thoughts but evildoing, which eventually leads to some facet of danger, and ending in some capacity of harm to someone or to something. But think about all of the people around the world who are angry about one thing or another. Anger is used by Satan to divide and conquer mankind against himself by one unjustifiable means or another. This is why it is so important to discuss this issue.

Stop and think about some of the people who you know are usually angry about one thing or another. Just imagine, these people are overcome with negative energy that could only result in some negative outcome leading to some facet of harm at the end of the day. Generally, people who harbor anger are not morally rational, not morally understanding, not at peace, not complacent, and are generally not friendly. These are mean-spirited people with a chip other shoulders about one thing or another of which many find it hard to forgive others for. This is how conflicts begin. This is how enemies evolve. This is how division is manifested, and is how unrest and wars become imminent in the world between people, societies, and nations. ANGER!

However, this is not to say that every person that gets angry fall in the evil category under the evil dynamic, because there are times that everyone gets angry about something. Even the most loving, moral, humble, and kindest people in the world have a tendency to get angry about things. The key is knowing how to rationalize and forgive. This is why the anger of the moral segment is met with reasoning, understanding, compassion, and eventual forgiveness. They don't harbor hatred, but are quick to forgive based on moral reasoning and respecting the intelligent fact that we live in an imperfect world with imperfect people.

Anger is short-lived by the moral people because it is not in their nature to retain negative energy or evil thoughts. Their anger is merely a temporary reaction to some facet of injustice that is shocking to their conscience, because they generally oppose evildoing and the works of the immoral. From their anger they seek justice. And rightfully so, to get justice sometimes it takes opposition, which eventually leads to violence, war, and destruction, which are all still characteristics of Satan and the evil dynamic, nonetheless. The difference is that the anger of the moral is to fight against injustices being done to humanity by the unjust. In wars of this nature, God assures that the just will prevail because He stands for justice, while Satan stands for injustice.

The anger by the moral is a reaction to those things that are definitively wrong, which are bad, evil, and things that are harmful to others. The anger of the moral is in rightful defiance against evildoings of one kind or another that infringes on civil and human rights of others. In any event, until justice is restored as it should be, moral people will not be happy or at peace, and will seek ways to rid injustices, which makes the moral definitively right, because they seek to harm no one at the end of the day. The moral simply wants justice and peace!

The truth of the matter is that nothing good is ever manifested or produced from the state of anger, which substantively makes anger the number one emotion utilized by Satan to bring destruction and ruin to mankind everywhere in existence. Understanding this truth is very important, because this understanding will allow you to reflect, to think about, and to truly rationalize about who people really are when considering the totality of his or her true character after all is said and considered.

If you have friends, family members, associates, or even if you meet strangers who are generally angry or mean-spirited individuals; this is clear proof that these people are under the authority and control of Satan. It means that they are not people of God. It means that they are generally not moral people. It means that they are generally not forgiving people. It means that they are potentially violent people. It means that they are harmful people unless they repent and change from their evil ways. It means that these people are grounded in negative energy that deprives someone of something instead of adding anything positive or of substance to the lives of others.

Just imagine, this one single emotional state of anger could manifest all of these evil and destructive characteristics among us. Despite this truth, society generally treat anger as just another walk in the park that is without any significance. Angry and racist political leaders in America are merely perceived as ordinary folks, despite fashioning their legislative agendas, laws, and policies based on bias perspectives, hateful feelings, and negative emotions; all manifested out of anger and hate, which are states deriving from the evil dynamic.

This substantively tells us that all of the legislation, laws, and policies that angry politicians have effectuated in the society were all manifested to our disadvantage by no other than Satan the devil himself. This is merely because we have not scrutinized or delimited the evil dynamic for what it truly is amongst us. We have minimized the relevance of Satan and the evil dynamic that thrives to destroy us through anger, which manifests hatred, violence, and war amongst humanity.

Let's be real; look at the vast majority of leaders within the Republican regime. I mean, truly consider all said above herein, and seriously think about the true character of most of these people. Look at how angry and mean-spirited Donald Trump is. Look at how angry and mean-spirited Jim Jordon is. Look at how angry and mean spirited the vast majority of Trump supporters are period. Look at how the vast majority of Republican leaders are period!

This is evidence of the presence of Satan, people. Anger is proof of the evil dynamic, and it is proof that these people are not of God. And if they are clearly not of God, why are their concerns, agendas, complaints, and propositions even being recognized, being treated as significant, and why are their issues being perpetrated & disseminated in the mindsets and lives of the society through journalistic platforms? It is because they too are merely Satan's puppets to keep the evil dynamic afloat? What other conclusion are we to reach?

Let's be real, people! Satan and the evil dynamic is in power, and has enthralled the nation through propaganda, deception, and orchestrated lies that are speciously designed to hold the people in bondage, in poverty, and in unending oppression by taking away jobs, by cutting out funding for several worthy causes, and by making unprecedented first-time changes in how the American government has run its orderly affairs in the nation over the last 200 years without any disruption. And this is specifically true for the fate of the Black American, who is facing the most catastrophic threat to his livelihood than any other people in the American society, after all he has been through over the course of America's history without any reprisal or conciliation for his atrocities.

The True Disposition of the Black American

When it comes to race relations in America, what bewilders me more than anything else is when whites get angry at Black Americans for repeatedly complaining about racism, despite that the essence of over 90% of black disputes are clearly and rightfully grounded in racism all the while, as they should. In other words, whites are quick to blame blacks of playing the race card, when the race card is the only true card to play at the end of the day, when considering all of the facts underlying the specific issue that may be under dispute, which will more than likely point out and expose the truth surrounding some audacious wrongdoings done by whites to blacks. They don't want to hear about or face the truth. And whenever blacks bring the truths to them they are quick to shut it down by accusing blacks of unfairly playing the race card. But the only card the Black American is left to play is the race card, because it is the only true card in the game after all others have been repeatedly played to his disadvantage.

In countless cases like this, the racist does everything in his or her power in efforts to dismiss, to avoid, or to disregard the evident truth exposing the evildoings they have done to Black Americans for centuries without facing any consequences. The truth is eating away at their conscience so severe, until they have even resorted to making attempts to eradicate Black History from school establishments completely. Whites are ANGRY at the Black American because he won't shut up and be quiet about the injustices done to him in past and present history. Merely because he won't be quiet about the injustices done to him, the black man is outright hated! Let's just be real about it and stop beating around the bush.

The truth is that all of the injustices done to the Black American over the nation's history manifested from the evil dynamic, ruled by Satan the devil. Yes, the predicament and disposition of the Black American in America only resulted from evildoing, hatred, and deliberate injustices manifested by immoral people - (evildoers)- who are led under the influences of Satan and the evil dynamic that is the nucleus of this book. At this point in America's history everyone knows what the Black American went through, but many still don't understand or respect the fact that in the aftermath of his slavery holocaust there were adverse mental, emotional, and repressive illnesses that actually shaped, fashioned, and formed a distasteful Black American culture that had no choice but to differ from the rest of the nation. And

116

because of his distasteful culture, the Black American is consequentially denigrated to date.

The entire black predicament was never resolved after hundreds of years of oppression, because the Black American was never given any reparation to accommodate for his drastic losses and historical setbacks. Those losses and setbacks engendered real mental, emotional, and physiological damages to black livelihoods of which White America never acknowledge, refuse to acknowledge, never cared about, nor ever made any concessions to do anything about for so long, until such deficiencies became normal and accepted traditions in black culture. This resulted in an array of mental and emotional damages that led to substance abuse, alcoholism, and the incentives for criminal insurrection for which Blacks are stigmatized, detested, and persecuted consequentially.

Despite this obvious impairment resulting from their own liability without any restitution, white America continue to disparage the Black American because his behavior, because his psychological temperament, because his values, because his propensity to fight against injustices, and because his overall standards of life is not equivalent to their own spoiled, stress free, stolen wealth, and unrealistic expectations that blacks should conform to their customs and ways of life. This is the kind of evil of which I am writing about that motivates the exposure of Satan and the audacity of the evil dynamic.

Think about it; what type of person would think to him or herself, "Hey, how about we travel to Africa and start kidnapping black people. We could then bring them to America and force them to work for whites without paying them anything?" What kind of mindset or mentality would even entertain such an evil thought from the outset? Certainly not a moral or Godly mindset would entertain such a thought. In fact, a moral mindset would not even think of such nonsense in the first place. The truth is that only an immoral and evil person would entertain such an idea, which paints the true image of who the former slaveowners were. Not only that, but all who agreed with their perspectives, and all who conformed to their slave-oriented traditions were all immoral and evildoers as well. Can this be realistically denied? No, because the facts and the truth is etched, recorded, and established in historical records that could never be erased, although the evildoers are now making efforts to erase history by removing black history from school establishments. Just imagine that!

The saddest thing about the Black American's predicament is that today he is expected to perform in his economical livelihood equivalent to whites and others who are non-afflicted, despite that the government and society are already aware that Black Americans were never given any reparation in order to do so. They already knew he could not equally compete in the economical game of life. They already knew that he had no political power, no control, no influence, no unity, no resources, no education, and entirely no economical base to even come anywhere close to competing or subsisting in his livelihood equivalent to whites. Think about that! Here we have whites, who kidnapped, enslaved, heaped up billions and trillions of dollars from the kidnapped slaves, raped and abused the wives and children of the kidnapped slaves, hung and burned black men and women slaves who were kidnapped, and then after the Emancipation that allegedly freed the kidnapped slaves; they then denied them any civil or human rights, denied them any reparation for centuries of atrocities, denied them decent housing, prevented them from obtaining bank loans or mortgages to own their own properties, prevented them from voting, and on and on. Yet, whites are angry at the Black America today because he is not performing in his livelihood and quality of life equivalent to the White American's expectation. Consequentially, he is detested, discriminated against, disparaged, ridiculed, mocked, and persecuted. All of this because he does not ethically, mentally, or economically perform in the society as do whites, according to their self-centered, independent, and unrealistic expectations.

Just the mere expectation of the Black American to function equivalent to whites in the American economy, derives from both sick and evil-minded rationalizations by unrealistic, delusional, and hateful whites who are clearly of Satan and the evil dynamic of which I write. Yet, these are the types of sick mentalities in political governments that are instituting unfair laws and policies that are adversely affecting the quality of life for the pervasive Black American community in America today. These are examples of the mentalities that are influenced under the evil dynamic, which are proactively working today in the mindsets of those who are secreted in Republican offices and places of power and authority without obvious detection, until lately.

Meanwhile, Black Americans have forgiven the past misdeeds of whites for the atrocities of slavery, despite complaining and revolting against the injustices of many ignorant and confused bigots who still carry stubborn racial hatred in their minds and hearts as I write. Unfortunately, President Donald Trump is one of those stubborn racists, who remains the biggest threat to the

Black American's safety and welfare than any other President in American history. Even though he himself has openly admitted that the American society was unfairly built from the backs of Black Americans without pay, he still refuses to show respect or to make conciliation between American blacks and Whites. I can see if he did not know, realize, or fully understand; but he intelligently knows, and still refuses to let up on the racial oppression. How much more evidence is needed to conclude that this man is Satan in the flesh?

Despite understanding that Black Americans are only 14 percent of the American population, Trump still continues to support racist policies and propositions presented by himself and other racists politicians that are clearly devised to bring harm and tribulations in black lives. For example: consider Project 2025, which is a Republican oriented plan, administratively designed to set the progress of Black Americans back 250 years of past struggles, where over history blacks fought ceaselessly for equal civil and human rights through rigorous revolts that led to white violence and countless murders of black lives. We only have the evil dynamic to blame for these injustices, which should be publicly recognized as such, by pointing out and identifying the specific immoral culprits operating in political offices at the behest of Satan and the evil dynamic.

It is time to face the truth. The evil empire has taken full control of American politics, and are now making it apparently clear that hatred, division, and war is more favored in the affairs of the nation over love, unity, and peace on behalf of Black Americans. Everyone knows the Black Americans are victims of historical oppression that was intelligently planned, which was catastrophic and knowingly injurious to black livelihoods for hundreds of years in the nation without equality of justice, life, or liberty. This is all proof of the evil dynamic, which is definitively wrong because black folks have never harmed any whites at anytime in history to warrant such atrocities. The only harm that blacks have done to whites was from some obvious retaliation which pushed them to take harmful measures.

Despite being painted as evil, violent, criminal prone, and dangerous people; evidence and facts are clear that Black Americans are not violent, not evil, nor troublesome people to any extent at all. Yet they still suffer as a result of the established propaganda, nonetheless. The truth is that Blacks are autonomously inclined to react with aggression and rightful resistance to ongoing injustices through rightful revolt, - (*that is erroneously labeled as trouble-making*), for which they are consistently denigrated and unjustly persecuted for as a consequence.

All of these tribulations against blacks are merely due to the evil dynamic that is captivated in the hearts and minds of immoral and bigoted whites in America. These demons simply will not allow blacks to live peacefully, no matter how complacent or law abiding blacks are. Let's be real; all of this is the work of Satan, who needs to be intelligently called out through the identity of those specific immoralists operating in American government under his control and authority. He needs to be called out by the true name, Satan, and this should be done and recognized all over the world to attest an understanding of who Satan really is.

DEI Hiring

Another critical injustice that deserves serious attention and discussion, surrounds DEI, which stands for *diversity, equity, and inclusion.* This is a hiring practice designed to create a diverse and equitable workforce recognized as "DEI hire." Personally, I think that the term is too confusing, unclear, and not direct enough so that everyone could clearly understand its' substantive meaning without any confusion. The term basically require job employers to meet quotas for hiring racial and ethnic minorities, women, or citizens with disabilities in the workplace, which should be proportioned to whites and other privileged people to avoid the impropriety and appearance of job discrimination. I don't know who came up with the term, but they should have simply came up with a SDABA - (Stop Discriminating Against Black Americans) bill. Instead of burying the truth with the DEI logic, it should have gotten straight down to the point so that it is made plain and simple for what it is truly saying.

In any event, the DEI bill was too fair, was too right, was too productive, and was too just for President Donald Trump and his cohorts to leave alone. Too many black people, immigrants, the handicapped, women, and others were employed with decent paying jobs to take care of their families without any hindrances. Just as Satan hates to see people complacent and at peace, Trump and his followers saw fit to eliminate DEI hires, and immediately after taking office he fired Black Americans from their DEI hired positions without any hesitation or prior warnings whatsoever. Who would conduct this type of merciless activity; a Godly person, or an evil person? Be real with yourselves, and perceive this man for who he truly is; an agent of Satan the devil. Please stop sugar coating the evidence, some of you!

This was merciless deprivation, disrespect, and a clear show of racial hatred without any sugar-coating. Despite this obvious truth, white men and women claim that the DEI hiring process is reverse discrimination against them, to which Trump agrees. We all know that whites have never faced any hardships in America, but are the ones who relentlessly subjected Black Americans to the longest, harshest, and the most painful hardships than any other human being upon the face of the earth could ever endure. And they did this without ever paying any reparations for the injuries they know they caused. This was evil, and is nothing more than the work of Satan and the evil dynamic.

It is evil for any person to disregard this historical truth, but yet seek to make it even harder for the Black American atop of the devastating injury already done to him without any reparation to ever uplift himself since Emancipation. Even more sickening is the fact that Black Americans only comprise of 14% of the American population, and whose income is a jaw dropping 33.3% less than whites. How much unfair could it be for Black Americans in the employment industry? This is why DEI was a fair system of reprisal for the unresolved injustices that Blacks have undergone in America for hundreds of years. But for some reason, Conservative whites and others have resorted to assert that DEI hires is reverse discrimination against them, despite that they are privileged, favored, and have always been dominant in all spheres of the economy and jobs industries. Let's just call it for what it truly is: race hatred, which is nothing more than the hateful and evil misconduct orchestrated by Satan and the evil dynamic.

Congresswoman Jasmine Crockett And Revelation of The Evil Empire

As this book seeks to expose the evil dynamic for what it truly is, and how it is working in the mindsets and lives of immoral segments; our reflection on Jasmine Crockett and her encounters with several Republican leaders gives us all the evidence that is needed to conclusively affirm that Satan is now in full political control of the American society.

First of all, we must bear in mind to consider the relevance of moral versus immoral people, Satan, and the evil dynamic. We must understand and keep in mind that there are two distinct characteristics in these two different types of people, as already made clear in prior discussion. The moral is loving, kind, considerate understanding, compassionate and helpful, among other good attributes. These are the characteristics that makes moral people considered to be good natured people. It is because they are Godly people, despite not being perfect people. Moral people are perceived to be righteous because they tend to help us as oppose to harming anyone, providing if they had to make a choice between the two options.

127

Before getting into the heart of this discussion, it is also very important likewise to understand the relevance, the nature, and the characteristics of immoral people. Immoral people are hateful, unkind, inconsiderate, uncompromising, and harmful to others in some capacity, among other evil things, as already elaborated on in prior discussions. Immoral people are seen as unrighteous because they tend to harm people as opposed to helping others, provided if they had to make a choice between the two options.

Do yourself a favor and research the varying differences and meanings of moral versus immoral people. You will find that one belongs to the good dynamic, while the other belongs to the evil dynamic. What makes them different is because of their good or evil characteristics, as far as their views, their ideals, their perspectives, their sentiments, their values, their rationales, and their behaviors and so forth. Because each dynamic hold contrasting dispositions adverse to each other, it is only fair to make a comparative analysis to determine what or who is right from wrong. This is because both cannot be right. If both good and evil are equally right, then there is no substantive meaning to anything in this life. But there is substantive meaning to life, and there are definitive rights from definitive wrongs in life. And when we identify something that is wrong, there is a moral obligation to condemn the wrong in the interest of truth and justice. If you care nothing for truth and justice, then put this book down now and go on about your business, because without truth and justice, we all may as well lie down and die anyway! Without truth and justice, there is no peace, there is no cause, no purpose, no meaning, no rationale, no reasoning, nor any foundation to justify anything in this world without embracing truth and justice as the principles of righteousness! Truth is a manifestation from proven facts. And once truth is established, only the truth could restore justice in any situation. Truth and justice equals righteousness. Righteousness is at the core of God's judgment against all conditions, circumstances, things, and people. So, there we have it; truth, justice, and righteousness. TJR; these are the most supreme fundamentals governing the entire essence of humanity. To deny any of these fundamentals to others is to deny God and His entire purpose for manifesting the human race.

What I am about to expose herein below, will clearly reveal that there are very dangerous people operating in America's government who has willfully, knowingly, intelligently, and deliberately denied these most essential fundamentals to the just without regard for truth, without regard for justice, without regard for righteousness, and without regard for God. The question now is: What should happen to people of this evil nature? How are we to deal with people of this evil nature?

Having understood this, let's now take a look at Congress woman Crockett versus all of the members of the Republican regime and others associated with the Republicans with whom she has encountered conflicting disputes and/or differences with. An analysis of these quarrels has deciphered out who is who, what is what, and why and how Satan himself has captivated the hearts, the minds, and the souls of these evildoers who are entrusted to control the fate and the political destiny of our lives in America.

Now think about this; based on what you have seen, know, or heard of Jasmine Crockett; would you say that she is an immoral person? Think about these questions carefully. Would you say that she is an evil person? Would you say that she is a hateful person? Would you say that she is a person that goes around lying? Would you say that she is a violent person? Would you say that she is a deceitful person? Would you say that she is generally an angry person? Although she has a right to be, given the way she is unfairly treated. But I think she pretty much has her temperament under control, given the circumstances. And would you say that she is a person without any love, understanding, or compassion?

I already know the answer to these questions, which is NO! She represents none of these negative characteristics. And if she does not represent any of these ugly characteristics, then why is she hated so severely by Donald Trump, the Republican regime, and countless others who are embraced by the Republican regime? Who would hate a non-violent, moral, and intelligent person who is merely fighting against injustices? Ask yourself this question! Why would a person of this moral nature be hated by anyone? Think about that! A person who only fights for justice, which is one of the most fundamental principles underlying humanity's inclination for peace and happiness everywhere on earth. She could not play a more vital role on behalf of the oppressed, the underrepresented, and people who are in need of political representation.

Although she is not perfect; Jasmine Crockett is a moral woman. A review of her past shows that as a young attorney, she fought for justice for those who could not even afford attorney fees. She put her life on the line standing up for what is right, regardless of the money. Her track record shows this and a long host of worthy causes that she has stood up for in the interest of truth, righteousness, and justice! She has proven herself to have integrity, respect, and prudence to do the right thing without any selfish motives. All she wants is righteousness and justice for those treated unfairly. What is wrong with that? That is what is in her DNA, what is in her heart, and what is in her soul as a moral individual and apparently a true child of God. This does not mean that she does not sin, that she is perfect, or that she is beyond reproach. I am only emphasizing that from what we have seen, witnessed, and know, she has presented herself as a moral person of integrity, and that's all we need to know.

She has both demonstrated and proven that she is not evil, which clearly proves that she is a servant of righteousness. Now, ask yourself, who opposes God and the righteous people that He has chosen? I am sure that you already know the answer to this question! No other than Satan the devil, who is the angry one, who is the evil one, who is the vengeful one, who is the untruthful one, who is the violent one, who is the treacherous one, who is the dishonest one, who is the deceitful one, who is the contentious one, and who is the antagonistic one who continually agitates and keep unnecessary strife stirring in the air about one thing or another amongst the human race! Does this remind you of anyone? These are the types of minds, spirits, and souls who are in adversity with Jasmine Crockett. What should this tell you?

As I think about Jasmine Crockett, I think about how many conflicting and heated debates she has encountered with various angry and mean-spirited people of the Republican regime, and how she has been persistently condemned and criticized for no realistic basis. Donald Trump stated that she is definitely a low IQ person. Then on another occasion, he called her a "Lowlife." He hates her with such horror, he even encouraged his attorney general, Pam Bondie, to somehow have her arrested. Through attempted intimidations, unfounded accusations, and unjustifiable threats without any substantive foundation or reasoning; even Supreme Court Justice, Amy Coney Barrett concocted a frivolous cause to have her arrested. Wonder why?

I will tell you why: It is because Jasmine has the audacity to fight for justice and righteousness, of which Satan hates to the core. That is why she was treated this way! She is hated because she opposes wrongdoing and injustice. She is hated because she is not afraid to speak up about it. She is hated because she is a black woman who refuse to fall in line and conform to the evil dynamic that is controlling the totality of the Republican regime and its followers. I am certain that it is no other than God Himself that is using Jasmine to decipher out and expose the satanic demons who are attempting to overthrow Democracy and American justice! Let's thank God for her!

Let's now consider the only Black American man sitting in the United States Supreme Court, Justice Clarence Thomas. Because of her integrity and zeal for justice as a Congresswoman, Jasmine investigated and exposed impropriety and misconduct done by Clarence Thomas, who she revealed had received over 4 million dollars in gifts and undisclosed luxury trips, despite being required by law to disclose such tainted gifts, but speciously failed to do so. In retaliation, he did all that he could to destroy her career, but to no avail because she stood her grounds with more surprised on-hand evidence exposing even more orchestrated corruption in government by Thomas and others.

Not only did she have run ins with Trump, Bondie, and Clarence Thomas; but equal conflicts with Jim Jordon; Karoline Leavitt; Nancy Mace, who even threatened to take a fight outside; Marjorie Taylor Greene; Governor, Greg Abbott, Stephen Miller; Supreme Court Chief Justice, John Roberts; Justice Elena Kagan; Director of the FBI, Kash Patel; Jeanine Pirro, House Speaker, Mike Johnson; Shawn Hannity; and many others who are supportive of the Republican regime; all who hates her to the core without entirely any just cause. If these are not all of Satan's people, then who are they? What more evidence is needed to prove who these people really are?

The only cause that any of these people have for opposing Jasmine Crockett is because they are evil, hateful, and immoral people who simply oppose truth, who oppose righteousness, and who oppose justice. How much more proof is required for us to identify the characteristics of Satan?We already know his characteristics. We already see his characteristics in Donald Trump and all of his above supporters. We already know this by merely seeing the anger, from their mean-spirited personalities, and from their intimidating gestures and attempts to somehow frame Congresswoman Crockett, who is innocent, non-threatening, and who is simply doing the job of standing up for justice, for which she was elected to do. This truth must be acknowledged and talked about. It is time that the evil dynamic be confronted for what it truly is, and time for those to be exposed who are incapsulated under its' principalities.

All of these above-mentioned immoralists have opposed and have shown clear hatred and unfair disdain for Congresswoman Crockett. Despite their attempts to entrap her, she has proven on each occasion of conflicting dispute to be a person of morals and integrity. She has proven that she only fights for justice in contradistinction to opposing injustices and organized corruption clearly being perpetrated by Donald Trump and the Republican Regime. What does this tell you about these types of people against whom she is contending? What does this tell you about their integrity? What does this tell you about those who hate others for telling the truth? What does this tell you about their underlying motives, when they fight against a person who only seeks justice and righteousness? What does this indicate, where it is clear that they show no love, no compassion, or any care for the less fortunate and people facing dire hardships, poverty, sicknesses, and other societal dilemmas that are beyond their capacity to change or to control?

This evidence clearly proves and unequivocally tells us that these are all of Satan's children, who were embraced, indoctrinated, and influenced under the evil dynamics to oppose the truth, to oppose righteousness, to oppose justice, and to oppose God. Given this type of irrefutable evidence as clearly documented and exposed; how else could anyone describe the true nature of who Trump and other associated members of the Republican regime really are? Would you conclude that any of these people are moral, of God, or display any Godly characteristics of any sort? Let's be fair and reasonably objective in answering these questions to yourself. Think about it!

Where is any of their compassion? Where is any of their love? Where is any of their integrity? Where is any of their humanitarianism? Where is any of their forgiveness? Where is any of their sympathy? Where is any of their morality? Where is any of their fairness? Where is any of their respect? Where is any of their dignity? Where is any of their honesty? Where is any of their righteousness? Where is any of their zeal for justice? Where is any of their consideration? Now just imagine; they have none of these Godly or moral characteristics whatsoever! Out of all these moral ethics, we cannot find entirely one good characteristic in none of these Republican officials or their associates. Yet, these are the people who are in charge of running our nation! We are in serious trouble, people! Remember, the United States Constitution was drafted to help us; not to harm us. This is why it is favored by God. Yet, because we have placed God and Satan on the same level of politics reasoning under the Constitution, the Constitution is now subject to be tainted with corruptive reasoning by Satan.

The evidence could be no more clear to prove that Trump and his followers are all Satan's people. This evidence also proves that not one of these people possess any characteristics of a moral or Godly person, which is self-evident in their statements, in their sentiments, in their attitudes, in their policies, in their characters, and in their political dispositions, which has clearly proven to harm others, rather than helping all the people under their province. Think about the angry, ugly, and mean-spirited disposition most of these angry people displays. Remember how I spoke in prior discussion about the relevance and implication of anger, and about how anger is Satan's number one mechanism of destruction? Think about members of the Republican Party of which you are familiar. Now consider the state of anger and how many of these people you have personally witnessed in their rage and angry states of minds.

These angry dispositions were revelations! Such anger and rage results from nothing more than evil thoughts, from hateful thoughts, from angered thoughts, from violent thoughts, from vicious thoughts, and from vengeful thoughts seeking to harm someone, somehow, for some reason that should have been forgiven, which is greatest commandment in the Bible, rather than keeping such negative energy bottled up inside waiting to explode at the behest of Satan and the evil dynamic.

None of these above characteristics are Godly or moral thoughts. Yet, these are the preponderance of the facial expressions, mean-spirited gestures, and overall negative body language that exposes who these people really are. They cannot hide from themselves. How often do you see people of the Republican regime smile, make friendly gestures, or show any true love or respect to anyone, aside from other demons amongst themselves?

Look at Jim Jordon; a mean spirited angry man who always carry a beef on his shoulders about one thing or another. He doesn't even realize it, but God is watching him! Look at Donald Trump; a complaining, angry, finger-pointing, mean-spirited, and very unkind man, always with a perpetual beef on his shoulders about something that is not even his business. These are not Godly or moral characteristics, people. In fact, take a closer look at nearly all of the Republicans and their psychological temperaments. You will find no love, no friendliness, no warmth of heart, nor any compassion in any of these people. You will only find firmness, coldness, seriousness, meanness, stiffness, and dryness in their character and mental temperaments. These are cruel characteristics. No matter how hard an evil person tries to hide his or her true identity, one's body language, facial expressions, and overall temperament reveals who they truly are. No one can escape from themselves! These are very vicious, cold, cruel, evil, and extremely dangerous people based on the facts; not hearsay or rhetoric that is merely blowing in the wind. We need to understand the evil dynamic for what it truly is! The very nature of these people is to harm others, as is clearly seen in their firm policies, in their causes, and in their mental states of persistent negative energy. Evidence that these people are of Satan the devil is more self-evident when considering how Trump coached the January 6th mob the attacked the Capitol. Those people were angry, violent, enraged, and destructive. These are all characteristics of Satan and the evil dynamic. None of their behaviors were of God or of a moral nature whatsoever. Trump incited such behavior by telling the crowd "You have to fight like hell."

The bottom line is that the chips have already been played by Trump and the Republican Regime, which clearly reveals established facts; which results from established evidence; which derives from established and filed records; which contains racist, bias, and discriminatory laws, bills, and harmful policies; which were signed into law by a hateful, mean-spirited, angry, and narcissistic United States President, Donald J. Trump; which was speciously done at the behest of the evil dynamic; which is ruled by Satan, who the entire world recognize as the devil. It is time to confront Satan

What I am endeavoring to establish is that: 1) These are immoral people in the nation's White House, who are operating under the evil dynamic ruled by Satan, which is based on factual evidence of the harm, unrest, and racial division that could only be instituted by the evil dynamic; 2) That the revelation and study of the evil dynamic, of Satan, and of immoral people who are motivated under Satan's influence, should be a matter of public awareness and education; and 3) That before people are permitted to hold political offices, each candidate should face public scrutiny and examination, relative to a help or harm analysis, to be established by Congress pertinent to new provisions of law under the Constitution, which will serve as a basis to analyze, to scrutinize, and to ascertain moral from immoral candidates seeking political and other affairs where people's livelihoods, freedom, and civil & human rights are at stake under the nation's Constitution.

The time has come for us to make definitive determinations between the good versus the evil segment controlling political and economical affairs in the nation as a standard way of life. It is time to make definitive determinations between what is right versus what is wrong ethics underlying political policies and objectives to minimize societal unrest. It is time to make definitive determinations by which to distinguish between immoral versus moral people, as a basis to restrict the immoral from having any societal power on the basis of its' innate harm to mankind. And as a basis to establish compassion, unity, love, and peace in the nation, as paradigms of justice to hopefully encourage moral servitude and peaceful human relations across the earth. This is a moral war led by the Holy Spirit of God, against the immoral assault on humanity led by Satan and the evil dynamic, which is responsible for every conflict confronting humanity everywhere on earth.

Conclusion

I carefully chose the title of this book to address a specific a concern that had always bothered me about life and the many complexities preventing peaceful human relations in America and in the world. As an artist, a humanitarian, and a devoted writer; my conscience was moved by a spiritual force that would not allow me to rest my mind until this subject matter was carefully thought out and documented once and for all relative to the true essence of the evil dynamic, of which I have come to understand, is responsible for all of the problems going on in the world!

Because I couldn't find any books that realistically addressed this issue, I was compelled to address this topic on my own interest and accord; with the wisdom, the discernment, and the guidance of no other than the Holy Spirit for the sake of justice. There is a God, and God is just. To deny justice is unjust and is to deny God. The only entity that denies God is the evil entity, ruled by Satan, who is the ruler of every injustice confronting humanity.

I boldly place this book in the hands of the world with humility, yet with confidence, trust, and assurance that it is seriously needed at this late stage of modern-day history to awaken sleeping souls, to give direction to lost souls, to untangle the minds of confused souls, and to serve as a compass for misdirected people from all walks of life in need of enlightenment about the most important issue confronting the livelihood of humanity everywhere on earth; Satan and the evil dynamic!

From reading this book, you should have reached the point of understanding by now that the evil dynamic is a genuine and tangible reality with adverse consequences to everyone everywhere within the ambient of its reach. That it is a demonic element with negative and destructive power that is invisible to the naked eye, yet visibly seen and painfully felt through its' devastated impact on the livelihoods, liberty, and quality life averse to men and women from all walks of life.

Hopefully, you will agree that the evil element is catastrophically destructive to mankind everywhere on earth. And that its fundamental nature and spiritual essence is totally and absolutely detrimental to all life. I am very optimistic that you will agree at this point, that it is the evil dynamic from which all of the worlds' problems stems, yet it's supremacy is not independently nor educationally seen or dealt with as a separate and distinct constituent to every disorder we face as a human race, as it should be recognized despite religion.

The truth is that no one has all of the answers to the worlds' problems. But we do have God's wisdom to see and understand the essence of who is behind the problems, the pain, the harm, the destruction, the division, the wars, and the senseless deaths of which we all dread in our lives over all other things in our plight to survive on this earth.

What is most disturbing is that racist, immoral, evil, and unrighteous politicians and their supporters complain, protest, and seek vengeance against others by one means or another, as if the world and the people in this life should be perfect. These evil people carry on as if they have no flaws themselves. And when we fail to be perfect or to live up to their unrealistic expectations, they insist that we face the cruel infliction of their own harmful retribution, rather than God's own judgment, despite that the Bible, of which they profess to honor, decrees that we should not judge others, but vengeance only belongs to God alone.

It is very unfortunate that we must contend with hateful, vengeful, and evil politicians who have no love or compassion in their hearts for all people. It is sad that there are those in political offices who hold racial prejudices, who are mean-spirited, who are selfish, who are unforgiving, and who are angry people for one reason or another; clearly exposing the obvious truth that there is no love or conciliation for peace found in their hearts, or in any of their reasonings.

This book should cause you to understand that Satan and the evil dynamic exist, are extremely dangerous, and that such an evil element should not play any role in political spheres of power, from which the overwhelming majority of people only look forward to for protection from harm, for protection for equal human rights, for protection for human civility, for freedom to pursue peace, happiness, and a good quality of life, as all other human beings are equally entitled to on this earth.

By my moral conscience led by the grace and holy spirit of God, I was inspired to write this book, with hopes that these words will inspire some to respect justice, that it will move others to show compassion and understanding, that it will enlighten the less empathetic to show love and compassion, that it will compel others to politically advocate in efforts to make productive change for all people, and with hopes that these words will inspire sympathetic politicians to pursue reformations in political affairs in efforts to make lawful concessions to eliminate evildoers, immoral people, and those enticed by the evil dynamic from holding responsible positions of power in any facet of governmental offices wherever life, liberty, and justice for the people may be threatened.

Whenever we encounter people who show no kindness, no love, no friendliness, no sincere smiles, nor any indication of true gentleness; evidence is revealed that the spirit of God is absent from these people. And if evidence reveals there is no Godly spirit in these people, know for certain that Satan and the evil dynamic is present instead. And Satan will by no means compel the immoral to do anything that is good at the outcome of any situation, under any circumstances, nor relative to any condition in this life whatsoever! Satan's only mission is to kill, to destroy, to create conflict, unrest, turmoil, division, chaos, and senseless violence against someone, somewhere, for some reason, for which there is no forgiveness, no compassion, no understanding, or love. Just imagine, these are the types of people currently in charge of running the nation in 2025, of whom we must contend with until 2029.

The only way that anything good could come from immoral people, is if they repent, denounce Satan, confess their sins, and change from their evil and wicked ways of life. Otherwise, evil and immoral people will always remain a threat to justice and peace, which is detested by God and moral mankind everywhere on earth. I realize that not everyone believes in God or Jesus from the Christian perspective of reasoning, and may therefore be reluctant to accept the metaphysical reasonings underlying the concept of this book. But what I do know is that nearly everyone believes there is a God, despite from whatever religious concept one's faith is predicated upon.

Although I respect everyone's personal religious preference, I myself believe in the principles and precepts of Jesus as taught under the New Testament of the Holy Bible, from where my inspiration, motivation, and preordination compelled me to write this book. For this reason, I cannot and will not deny Jesus or the doctrine that He taught, whether you may agree or not.

Let's from now on look at life from a different angle of reasoning, by educating ourselves to be more astute about the dynamics of Satan and the evil dynamic, despite religion, so that collectively we can reshape American culture to reflect a more peaceful, friendly, and productive nation on behalf of all people.

The Justice of Truth

One thing is for sure: the truth will never change, regardless of whoever tries to refute it. The truth needs no validation, it needs no help, it needs no support, it needs no approval, nor does it need any assistance to prove what it is. It is sincere, candor, honest, genuine, accurate, correct, right, valid, authentic, factual, actual, certain, legitimate, and is a matter of reality in the face of absolutely any controverting lies or opposition by anyone.

This book exposes the absolute truth about Satan, about the evil dynamic, and about specific people operating in political governments who are immoral and harmful to humanity, speciously working in the guise of Satan. It is true that Donald Trump is an evil man, when defining the meaning of the word evil and all of its associated characteristics. Define the word for yourselves, and then compare the characteristics of Donald Trump to the word evil and see what you come up with. The truth is what it is! It can not, will not, and does not lie!

It is true that Donald Trump and the Republican Regime's policies, bills, and political propositions are all harmful, depriving, divisive, self-serving, not in the best interest of the people, and are immoral when sincerely looking at their consequential nature. Look at their bills and policies themselves to see the essence of these truths, whereas there is an absence of help for the people in any of them, which is only how we can recognize the hand of God in any of their works. It is true that the hand of God is not recognized in any of the work or agendas of Trump and the Republican Regime. People can refute this truth all they want, but the evidence clearly shows this truth. What does this mean? It means that Satan is behind the activities of these people! Awaken, folks!

It is true that anger is an attribute of Satan, the devil, and that members of the Republican regime and others of their affiliations are pervasively angry people. The established facts, recorded evidence, analytical statistics, and millions of witnesses to this truth are all the proof we need. It is true that these are angry and violent people who are dangerous, who are evil, and who are harmful to others in the nation and in the world. These truths are relevant facts that are substantive and material to understanding how societal unrest, division, and racial conflict have prevented peaceful human relations in the nation and in the world. Deny the truth all you want; the facts are not going to change.

It is true that hatred is only of Satan, the devil, and those that he entices, and that President Donald Trump and those who support him are pervasively hateful and angry people. The proof is in their policies, in their statements, in their sentiments, in their stances, and could be ascertained by looking at the clearly evil people whom they are prone to support. The truth is what it is. They cannot escape the facts. No one can escape the truth of history once it is established. The truth is that these are all evil people who are under the influence of Satan and the evil dynamic that is currently controlling the political fate of the nation in 2025, right now!

It is true that the United States Constitution is a moral document that was written only for the good and help of the nation, and contains nothing of a harmful or evil nature. It is true that the Constitution does not deprive citizens of any rights, tangible or freedom, to pursue peace, happiness, and the liberty and equality of life. It is true that since President Donald Trump took office in the White House, several provisions of the United States Constitution have been challenged, disregarded, breached, and undermined without regard for the precedent laws and processes enacted through Congressional legislation for over two centuries without disruption or challenge.

It is true that the United States Constitution has utterly left an open door of opportunity for Satan and the evil dynamic to contend with the political affairs of the nation by default of the First Amendment and Equal Protection of Law Clauses, which permits Satan to retain the same rights as God under its provisions. It is true that the Constitution is a moral document with only moral intentions, yet now impeded upon by an immoral and evil President who is now changing the Constitution's moral ethics and good intent to help the people, to one that is of an evil nature to now harm the people.

It is true that under the leadership of Donald Trump, people are victims of deprivations, mass unemployment, racial discrimination, racial division, unlawful imprisonments, and victims of intimidation and threats for protesting and speaking out against injustices under their First Amendment Rights to the United States Constitution. It is true that there is no show of love, forgiveness, compassion, consideration, or conciliation in the character, personality, or ambience of President Donald Trump and his supporters to any extent whatsoever, which by and within itself affirms that he is not a man of God, as he claims to be.

It is true that Donald Trump has opposed, offended, disrespected, challenged, and/or made enmity with every person with whom he has ever dealt in some shape, form, or fashion. It is true that Donald Trump is not a friendly man, not a kind man, not a respectful man, not an understanding man, not a righteous man, not an honest man, and not a moral man. It is true that these are all truths that cannot be realistically refuted, except by lying with dishonesty and falsehoods, which is what only Satan does alone!

It is true that Black Americans have never experienced peaceful livelihoods in America without racial hindrances, job discrimination, false imprisonments, and Equal Rights violations, which have pushed black culture into recalcitrant behavior patterns for which they are repeatedly prosecuted. It is true that Black Americans are the most underprivileged and disadvantaged of all people in America because they were never granted any reparations to uplift themselves following the aftermath of the slavery holocaust, as other victims of atrocities were paid.

It is true that times have changed, and that America is now becoming the most evil nation on earth because of Donald Trump and the Republican Regime's negligence to show any love, respect, compassion, or help to all of the people. To be truthful, the United States Pledge of Allegiance does not conform to the reality of American democracy today, and should be changed to reflect the truth.

This is how it should truly be read to reflect the real reality today: "I pledge allegiance to the flag of the United States of America, only for immoral Republicans for which it now stands, one white nation without God, divided, without liberty or justice for all."

This is not an exaggeration, not a joke, nor some game in defiance of the nation's Allegiance. This is the actual truth of the United States of America's current state of affairs. Under the nation's leadership under President Donald Trump, we now find ourselves dominated by an all white Republican administration that does not honor the principles of God, that has created division amongst the citizens, that deprives freedom from innocent citizens, and that denies equal justice for all citizens.

These are all above truths that cannot be refuted, no matter how many ways or perspectives one may try to twist reality. Truth is what it is. It will never change to appease one's dislikes, discomforts, or misapprehensions. There is more than enough evidence to verify all of these above truths, and just because another person may dispute, oppose, or contest these truths, it will not change these truths!

It is true that this book is a challenge and a direct confrontation against Satan and the evil dynamic that is at the center of America's political domination and potential decline to sustain peaceful subsistence in the world.

Prayer for the People

Father God: in the precious name of Jesus and through the Holy Spirit, we humble our hearts to You, Who is the Highest, Who is the most Omnipotent, Who is the Most Powerful, and Who is the Only All-knowing Creator of humanity and all life known to the human mind. With all due respect, Father God, we plead to You to look down upon us in Your tender mercies, with Your unwavering grace, and with Your lenient favor; and help us to find peace and consolation in the midst of uncertainty and times of peril and confusion in America and throughout the earth, being led by Your adversary Satan and the evil dynamic, who are in direct defiance to Your Devine Principles and Authority.

Father God, Please let these words be acceptable and consecrated in Your sight and in Your presence. We need You now! Your adversary Satan is without realistic challenge, and has gained a foothold over the political affairs of the world, and is causing conflict, violence, destruction, war, and senseless death on earth right now. And without Your intervention, we are limited in our power or capacity to stop him, Lord. We need You now more than ever!

Merciful Jesus and King; You know that the words written herein this book is only intended to open the eyes of the world to see the truth behind the shield of Satan's deception, lies, falsehoods, and influential tactics orchestrated to mislead, deceive, and to captivate vulnerable, naive, and foolish men and women who are without spiritual guidance, without understanding, without discipline, or without the necessary wisdom to escape the clutches of Satan's grip. Forgive these people Lord, because they don't truly understand what they are doing,

Father God, in Your all-knowing wisdom, You know that the United States Constitution was an inspired document that was written for the good of humanity in all respects. You know that it was written from the moral consciousness men for the purpose of helping others, and nowhere under any of its provisions did it intend to bring harm upon the people.

But Lord, Satan has swiveled his way into the fundaments of the Constitution on Equal Protection and First Amendment Rights Clauses, through which he has placed himself Equal to Your authority, despite the Constitutions' good intent. Somehow and somewhere along the way, Lord, Satan has separated the power of the Church from the State, where he is not bounded by Your spiritual authority, which gives him the legal rights by man's laws to do anything he wants without regard for Your divine word or admonitions. We pray of You Father God, to intervene and make these crooked affairs straight for the betterment and to help the people. Father God, through news media miasma and organized propaganda, the people are confused, lost, misdirected, and are oblivious to see or to understand how Satan has achieved world dominance, influence, and control over the masses. We need for You to expose and stop him now, Father!

Father God, please consecrate this book, and let it serve to awaken those who need to be awakened. Let it move those to see beyond a brighter horizon who could not previously see this new dawn of understanding. Let it move moral politicians and others in authoritative positions to devise productive legislation, laws, and humanitarian processes to expunge Satan and the evil dynamic from having entirely any power, authority, or control over any political matters where people's lives, liberty, peace, and pursuit of happiness is at stake.

Merciful Father God, we place all of our burdens, problems, issues, concerns, and apprehensions at your feet, clearly knowing the we are without the power or wherewithal to do anything without You. Please accept, consecrate, and receive these words, Father. In the name of Jesus and through the Holy

Spirit, we humbly thank You Father for granting this petition and the substantive nature and meaning of every word expressed herein. Amen!

Comments so far:

"Finally, a book that sets the record straight about what is really going on! I now understand life from a whole different perspective. Thanks brother!" Anthony Justice Wright

"This book is long past due. There is no way anyone can read this book without coming to realization of something valuable, different, and new. I am amazed at this new found understanding! Thanks to the author. You really put a lot of serious thought into this book." Mary Lamar Johnson

"One of the wisest writers of all time! I mean, really. Now I clearly understand everything that is going on with religion and American politics. I really appreciate you for this book my friend!" Ralph O'Brien, Jr.

"This discussion is seriously needed in life." I wish someone would have told me about these things," Carolyn Beckman

Jeremiah Stubbs

"Just when I thought I had life figured out, then comes this book. It is God sent!" Jeff Stevens

"This is a book that everyone in the world should read." Barbara Holden

"This book is going to save the world." Robert Keenly

www.ingramcontent.com/pod-product-compliance
Lightning Source LLC
Chambersburg PA
CBHW060119260626
47160CB00005B/1939